BITTER JOURNEY

When Ord Fielder had to quit his farm, he hoped to find a new life in Travis County. So Ord, his wife, two daughters, brother-in-law and the mongol, Lou Julius, set out in two wagons. But it was destined to be anything but a peaceful journey as Bob Chapin and his unsavoury followers quickly made clear. Worse still was the appearance of the dangerous Tom Alyard. Soon a lethal terror was unleashed and survival became the name of the game.

FRANK SCARMAN

BITTER JOURNEY

Complete and Unabridged

LINFORD
Leicester

First published in Great Britain in 1999 by
Robert Hale Limited
London

First Linford Edition
published 2000
by arrangement with
Robert Hale Limited
London

British Library CIP Data

Scarman, Frank
  Bitter journey.—Large print ed.—
Linford western library
  1. Western stories
  2. Large type books
  I. Title
  823.9′14 [F]

  ISBN 0–7089–5626–2

Published by
F. A. Thorpe (Publishing) Ltd.
Anstey, Leicestershire

Set by Words & Graphics Ltd.
Anstey, Leicestershire
Printed and bound in Great Britain by
T. J. International Ltd., Padstow, Cornwall

This book is printed on acid-free paper

1

The stranger had come and gone. Not the first and not the last of his kind; but gone, as soon enough these farm people themselves would be gone. Yet this most recent rider had had about him a disturbing aspect. A life-ravaged man, no question about it, come in on a lean, black horse, a man whose cheekbones stood sharp, angling the planes of his face, and whose dark eyes looked out darkly from dark pits. A man with a full black moustache curving from his lips. All about him, all his clothing had been well kept but obviously was far from new, worn-looking, his black pants, his dark-blue denim shirt, his black leather vest, his black, shallow-crowned hat, its thongs hanging on either side of his face. Age? Hard to tell. Late thirties, certainly. Older, maybe.

The horse looked as though it had

travelled some ways. There was bedroll up behind the cantle, and a low-scabbarded repeating rifle with a battered, scratched stock. The man himself was armed, a thickly brassed shellbelt around his middle, a use-grimed, sweetly curved cedar handle of a pistol horned from his left hip, butt foremost.

Come seeking clean water for him and the animal. Given water, and given, as well, a meal of hot biscuits by those who, by this time, had little enough for themselves, he had been watched openly by a girl of maybe thirteen, watched covertly in a too-busy-to-be-looking way by another girl of seventeen or eighteen, striking, black-haired like the others, blue-eyed and long-lashed. Watched with a sort of kindly reserve by the homesteader himself and his comely black-haired wife. Watched, wet-lipped and blinking by a man with a deeply lined neck that was counting his seasons more accurately than was his boysmooth face;

middle-aged, with the wits of a ten year old. Orphan, taken under this roof years ago, out of Christian compassion. And observed most carefully by the farm-wife's brother, dark-visaged, mistrustful, full of a voiceless, brooding anger, one arm hooked over a roughly fashioned crutch, pants leg pinned up, no left foot.

And while, head bent to his meal, the stranger, who had given the name Tom Alyard, had offered no obvious impression of curiosity, he had none the less taken note of the elder girl, the one who had affected to ignore him. But mostly, he had watched carefully the comings and goings of the one-footed man whose scrutiny, not far short of challenging, had been plain from the time the man had come walking the black horse into the farmyard. It was a scrutiny that was to persist to the time the man pushed his chair back and rose from the table, took up his hat, went out and remounted. '*Right obliged, ma'am.*' Dark rider on a black horse, different, yet not altogether different from many another rootless man eternally on the move. And judging by the faint accent, once a Johnny Reb. That alone would not have endeared him to Henry Pedderson.

There were, however, matters of manifestly greater concern to this farm family than this one or any number of hard-faced, dusty drifters. This farm, as a farm, was finished. More than a year ago the market for its produce had begun the process of dying, from about the time the town of Bethane had not got the spur of the railroad that had been so confidently expected, and had itself begun withering away; so it, too, was now close to death, numerous of its buildings no more than sun-warped shells, tall weeds growing around them.

Other farmers had already gone. The Sawtells, the Ebers, the Caines. Seen off by banks and loan companies, only those possessions considered to be essential piled on to wagons along with men, women and children, all heading away, and only vaguely aware of where. Some better place. Surely there had to be one, better than the one they were quitting. So this family would be next, and last, to leave the Bethane area. Yet it had been their instinct to cling to their life here to the very last, to continue existing here, unwilling to make the final move off their land. No, not their land. Not any more. The bank's land.

Where the Fielders might move to was not a settled matter. The place they wanted to go to was a long way south-west, across some very difficult country, to Travis County in fact, where Ord Fielder's brother owned unencumbered land. Ord did not entirely relish the thought of going on down there in these circumstances, to kinfolks, like a beaten dog; but there was his wife, Hanni, to consider, and Sarah and Lilah. And his uncommunicative brother-in-law, Henry Pedderson. And the half-witted orphan, Lou Julius. Lou could never be abandoned now.

Having watched the man who had

come for water go riding quite slowly away, Ord Fielder could not prevent his thoughts going back to the incident of yesterday, the Bob Chapin visit. Sarah came walking from one of the outbuildings and into the barn. It had been Sarah, of course, who had been at the heart of it; Sarah whose presence had fetched the unappealing, stringy-whiskered Chapin, hat removed, his hair slicked down, doing his best to present himself as less foxy but not succeeding. Come seeking the pretty farm girl. Once a rancher, Chapin, until too much liquor and poor prices and even worse company had all combined to kill that enterprise. Hard to know how Chapin got by at all nowadays, considering all that and the company he was still keeping. The likes of Jack Drago, Ramon Sanchez and, from time to time, Joseph Small Bear; and young Clem Cotton, all of whom, at various times, had worked for Chapin on his C-Bar spread. Hanging around what was left of the town, now, that crowd, Chapin often included. But he had long sought after Sarah Fielder, Bob had; could not get her out of his mind for long. Day and night. So, at long last, he had come a-courting. Seriously. He had not been well received and he had not taken the rebuff at all well. The greenish, brown-shot eyes had shifted from Ord Fielder to the farmer's elder child, and colour had suffused the gaunt cheeks. Bob had wanted Sarah real bad, had drunk, eaten and slept the name of the girl for one hell of a long while.

Effectively, that was what set off the chain of events, this humiliation of Bob Chapin. The one thing that led to another. That, and the fact that Chapin's friends, or rather, the men he drifted around with, were all of a kind, a streak of viciousness not far beneath the surface, any one of them needing but the smallest affront, the nudge that would be enough to push him over into quick violence. A striking back at ill-fortune. Make some bastard pay. Anybody. This, with the possible exception of young Clem Cotton.

Sarah Fielder now thought that she, for one, would be glad to be shut of this place, and very glad indeed to be out of the squinty sight of Bob Chapin. He made her skin crawl. And she was well aware that in his final look, before he had gone stomping away to unhitch his bay horse and swing up into the saddle, there had been an unsettling mixture of agony and threat. It had been made worse, somehow, because he had spoken no hard words. It had been as though the holding in of anger had rendered him more dangerous. Unfinished business.

Henry Pedderson had seen it too, and had recognized it for what it was. Henry had had a good deal of experience of men such as Bob Chapin. And Henry himself knew all about vindictiveness. Chapin sure had turned rattlesnake dangerous, for clearly he was obsessed with Sarah Fielder.

Watched her every chance he got. (*'Ridin' by'*, *Miz Fielder*.) And Hanni had always taken the safest course, that of offering cool courtesy, balancing the dark glances of her brother, Henry, leaning on his crutch. Old soldier. Well, not so old at that. Soldier at sixteen. Farm boy, gone off to join the blue columns, singing. Before it all turned to shit. It had spared that old Henry, yet, sparing him, had sent back only a brooding, suspicious husk. And with only one foot.

In all of this, only the child-man, Lou Julius, accepted each day as it came, had a ready grin for all comers, tended the farm horses, hummed to himself and complained about nothing. Like a plump shadow, Lou, so they were not unduly surprised when, one morning, he was noticed, some fifty yards from the homestead, approaching a lone, wandering horse. A lean young roan, a filly, suspicious, rolly-eyed, yet stretching its long neck out when Lou drew near, presently going right up to it, comforting, crooning softly, then stroking the trembling hide.

Drying her hands on her apron, Hanni, standing in the yard doorway, watched him. She turned her head, looking back inside the kitchen. 'Where's Lilah?'

'Gone off on her own.' Sarah's light voice.

Hanni nodded, went on watching Lou and the unknown roan filly. Hanni sighed. For some reason her younger daughter had suddenly gone quiet at the prospect of leaving this farm. Born here. And survived. Not so the two sons who came after, buried near the treeline, yonder, dead before their first year was out. Now, in a matter of days indeed, they would be abandoned here. Hanni and Ord, Sarah, Lilah and Henry and Lou heading away. Most likely down into Travis County. Daring the badlands between here and that place. A lot of things would have to be left behind. No room for everything, with only two wagons and the six farm horses to haul them. Henry's property, wagons and horses. His contribution. But now, it seemed, Lou had acquired another animal.

Ord Fielder appeared, walking with the deliberate gait of a man who has long laboured on the land, tall, though a trifle stooped, forty-three years old, his once black hair greying at the sides, whipcord-hard limbs, large, awkward hands. He had stopped alongside Lou and reached out to touch the filly's nose.

'Brand on her?' Lou, grinning, comprehending, shook his round head. Even so, Ord walked all around, examining the animal. It was true. No brand. Ord stood, hands on hips. 'Somebody's had her.' A couple of stripes on her left flank. 'Taught her to stand quiet.'

Hanni came, and Sarah. Hanni said, 'We can't take her.'

Ord glanced at his wife. 'Tell Lou.' Lou's biglipped mouth had fallen open. Hanni looked at her husband, shrugged. Too soft where Lou was concerned. Gave in too easy. She walked back towards the house, holding up the hem of her old green skirt. Sarah stayed, stroking the filly, smiling at the beaming Lou.

The thirteen-year-old, Lilah, was down beyond a clump of cottonwoods some thirty yards beyond the huge barn, wandering along, a yellow straw between her teeth. In the day's warmth she had unbuttoned the top of her blue dress, and now with one small hand, lifted the weight of her long black hair from the back of her neck. Now that the day of departure must be drawing close, Lilah wanted to be by herself for a time. At first the excitement of leaving for places unknown had seemed appealing, but as day had followed day, the realization that all these familiar scenes would soon be behind her forever, had begun to sink in. She was unexpectedly saddened by the thought of leaving.

So engrossed was the young girl in these musings that she failed to notice the horsemen. They might have been here for some little while, sitting their saddles, watching her. At first, when she did notice them, she thought that Bob Chapin had come back, before realizing that these raggylooking, very dirty men were complete strangers. Their aspect was frightening. Lilah turned to head back for what she saw as the safety of the trees. That was when they moved. Even though she was running they caught up with her real fast. One of the riders leaned down and scooped her up. She let out one scream before a gloved hand fastened roughly over her mouth.

One scream, however, was enough. Ord heard it. Henry Pedderson heard it. Ord ran towards the trees. Hanni came quickly from the house, Sarah behind her. Henry, swinging along with remarkable speed with the aid of his crutch, was heading towards the house.

Lilah was kicking and squirming. The man who had taken her was having a lot of trouble holding her and control-ling the horse as well. The animal was screwing around and tossing its head, the man cursing it and cursing the fighting girl. The other two, on wheeling horses, were urging their companion to get moving. At that moment Lilah, the fabric of her dress ripping, fell free and went rolling through the bunch-grass. The horse was rearing and blowing.

At the edge of the trees, Ord Fielder appeared. One of the retiring riders drew a pistol and shot at him. Ord dropped, but had not been hit. Hanni and Sarah appeared. Ord yelled to them to go back. Lilah had not got to her feet, but whether it was because she was injured or simply terrified out of her mind, was unknown. A horseman shot again at Ord, smoke spouting from the pistol, but again the farmer was unharmed.

Henry Pedderson came into view. He stopped. Standing on one foot, he was resting a short-barrelled weapon with a brass-glinting frame across the top of his propped crutch. This firearm was one said to have been acquired by

Pedderson a while back, during one of his drinking and gambling sessions in one of the Bethane saloons. Every now and again Henry cut loose and when he returned to his brother-in-law's homestead, was always contrite for a time. It was a .44 Winchester Model '66 repeating carbine with a round, twenty-inch barrel, below which was a tubular thirteen-round magazine, and with a straight-grip stock. It weighed seven and three-quarter pounds. Henry, since bringing it home, had practised a lot with the weapon. Now he did not hesitate. Pistols had been fired. One of his young nieces lay among the long grasses, unmoving, maybe hurt badly. Or dead.

The carbine banged. The rider who had had hold of Lilah and who was now putting spurs to his quietened horse, was following the other two. So all were retreating. But this last man away was the unlucky one. He was whacked solidly in the back and punched forward over the horse's neck. The lead had smashed through lower vertebrae and exited through his belly. The man pitched off the horse and hit the ground hard and went rolling over and over like some discarded, broken doll. But this was a screaming doll.

Looking back, seeing what had befallen their partner, the other two went quirting away, the stray horse galloping along in their wake. Henry was tracking the fleeing horsemen with the rested carbine but changed his mind, lowered the weapon and shrugged the crutch into his left armpit with the unthinking skill of long custom.

The man who had been screaming had now ceased and was making only low groaning noises. Ord and Hanni went quickly to Lilah who was now getting to her feet, but when the Fielders discovered that she was frightened but little hurt, they crossed to where the shot man lay.

Nothing could be done for him. Where the lead had come out of his belly was an oozing mass of bluish intestines. Because they did not want to move him, Hanni fetched blankets. A rough, ragged, stinking man he was, his clothing greasy from being worn day in, day out. He was a total stranger, but they had seen his like before. Drifter. Two hours later he went drifting out of life. Two hours after that, in a roughly fashioned pine box they lowered him into the earth not far from where Henry had shot him off the horse. Ord marked the grave with a stake. Hanni said a prayer. Scowling, Henry stood off to one side by about ten yards. Sarah and the lip-hanging Lou came to watch but Lilah would not. Ashen-faced she lay on top of her narrow bed with her fingers tightly clenched.

To no one in particular, turning from the burial-site, Ord said, 'This whole goddamn' country's gone loco.' He might just as well have added, '*But no more. Tomorrer we're headin' away.*'

He did not know the half of it.

2

One of the Bethane saloons was still getting enough business to stay trading, but not much other activity was to be seen around town. Many stores and dwellings had been abandoned. In the saloon were stained tables, sawdust on the floor and behind the long bar an ornate but grimy mirror, a reminder of times more affluent.

Bob Chapin, however, was not in the long, smoky bar-room but in a back room where card players were sometimes to be found. Today there was only Chapin and a broad-faced man with stained and broken teeth, one Ramon Sanchez. Chapin had fetched a couple of bottles of rye, in no doubt that before long, other company would come walking in.

Chapin was in a black mood. He was now pacing around and making no secret of his deep resentment over the Fielder affair. Great humiliation had turned to burning anger. Sanchez, his flat face immobile, had heard a lot of this before, for he, with others, had long been aware of this man's obsession with — as she was spoken of out of Chapin's hearing — *the farm girl*. So Sanchez did not have much to say, but from under heavy lids, sat watching Chapin pacing back and forth, allowing him freedom to give vent to his displeasure.

'An' that bastard Pedderson, he was there, that one-foot ol' soldier-boy, hooked on that crutch an' sneerin'.' Chapin paused to stare at the implacable Mexican. 'By God, Ramon, one day, an' mebbe one day real soon, I'm gonna take that hobblin' shit an' hang his goddamn' hide on a pole!' Glass clinked as he paused and poured himself another shot. For his part, although he took good care not to say so at this time, Sanchez was unable to understand what the difficulty was. In his view, if a man wanted a certain female he simply took her. Nothing complicated about it.

Sanchez shifted slightly on his hard wooden chair. Middle-aged, he had deeply pouched, very small black eyes and a black moustache curving from his upper lip. There was a white, puckered scar on the left side of his jaw. He was clad in very dirty range clothing of poor repair and slung with a pistol that had a stag handle. His half-boots were old and cracked. From time to time he had appeared on the Chapin ranch, the C-Bar, when it had been more or less a going concern, before whiskey and rock-bottom beef prices had put an end to it. Now even though C-Bar was no more, Sanchez was somehow still around. Maybe it was a case of like meeting like, this acquaintanceship of him and Chapin. Along with one or two others. Unplanned associations, but with the suggestion, now, of permanence. Men of a similar stripe, on the lookout for opportunities to sustain themselves in what were turning out to be very hard times indeed. And there were now no restraints. The law, such as it was, did not any longer exist around Bethane.

Yet Chapin, today, could not get his thoughts beyond Sarah Fielder. It must be no more than a couple of days until she, with her family would leave the farm and head on out. To where, he did not know. Maybe the Fielders didn't either. So Chapin resumed his restless pacing and his cussing. It was when in this sort of mood, and drinking, that Bob Chapin could be dangrous and best left well alone. Unreasonable. Unpredictable. Willing to push to the limits and beyond.

Now Chapin stood with thumbs hooked in his belt, staring at an oblong of grimy glass, yet staring at nothing in particular; or maybe it was at the remembered face of the black-haired girl with her long lashes and cobalt eyes, her small waist and high breasts and her graceful way of walking, seemingly without any effort. Almost

21

fragile-looking, not coarsened by farm living, so an unusual young female in every way.

Sounds came from outside in the alley, sounds of some kind of disturbance. Blinking, Chapin came back to himself. Sanchez's chair scraped noisily as he stood up. There was a rickety side door. Chapin went to it and pulled it open, Sanchez going with him, one hand on the curved, stag handle of his pistol.

Two men were in the sandy, fly-darting alley, one a young fellow clad in range clothing, eyes reddened with drink. The other was part-Indian wearing a pair of yellow-striped, blue cavalry pants, a loose black leather vest over his bare chest, a folded red bandanna tied around his forehead, coarse dark hair hanging between his shoulder blades. A muscular man, his age could have been anywhere between thirty and forty. Joseph Small Bear, who had been on his way to join Bob Chapin and Ramon Sanchez and who, for some reason, had run afoul of a half-drunk cowboy.

Within the confines of the alley, these two were shuffling back and forth, the cowboy with gloved hands raised, Joseph Small Bear with his broad-bladed knife drawn. A pistol could be seen in the cowboy's waistband. That in all likelihood he was incompetent with the weapon, and even partly drunk, knew it, for so far he had made no attempt to pull it.

The hard-drinking cowboy in his supposedly pugilist's stance went shuffling backwards, for by now he must have known that, while the sight of the knife was disturbing enough, he had come up against a man who was highly skilled in its use. From the moment that Joseph Small Bear got the knife in his hand the cowboy had sobered somewhat. He backed off some more. The Indian, skin glistening under the open vest, moved lightly after him. Arcing around fast, the blade glinted, causing the cowboy to go leaping back, stumbling on the high heels of his boots, his face under his tall, wide-brimmed hat gone ashen. That was just about the time that all reason deserted him and he grasped the handle of the pistol and tugged at the weapon. It refused to come free at once, and Joseph Small Bear, almost dancing on his toes, slipped closer in, and this time the slicing blade striped the cowboy, opening his shirt, a fine incision immediately flushing with bright blood. A cry burst from the cowboy. He was still retreating, the Indian following with silky ease. Then the pistol, an old one, some kind of Colt, was jerked free of the waistband; but before it could be cocked, the knife was driven home, thrust savagely up under the middle of the other's ribcage, driving from the cowboy a kind of *huffing* sound. The knife was out, then in a second time. Out and in again. The pistol had swung wide of the holder's body, then the cowboy was down, his hat coming off, his riven shirt a mess of fresh blood, his mouth open, his eyes glazing over.

Joseph Small Bear stepped lithely away, wiping the blade on his own pants. The fallen man was making gurgling noises and a bloody froth was bubbling from his mouth. The Indian who had knifed him had turned away. He had lost all interest. If the man lying there was not dead he was not far off it. Flies were whirling, settling on him.

Bob Chapin and Ramon Sanchez had gone back inside. Joseph Small Bear followed them. He did not say what the dispute had been about and they did not bother to ask him. He helped himself to a shot of rye. They all drank.

Chapin asked, 'Seen Jack?' Jack Drago. Expected sooner or later.

Joseph Small Bear shook his head slightly. 'Nope. See las' night.'

'Jack, he be with Rosie,' Sanchez opined. Rosie Benato. One of the whores at the Daneman House. Red headed, feisty, the only one among them who would take no shit from

25

Drago and who, astonishingly, Drago had never struck. As a rule, Drago was very bad with women.

They drank and talked some more. It was as though the dead or dying man in the alley had never existed. With his brown-bean eyes, Joseph Small Bear had been studying Bob Chapin. Without being told he could see that it must have gone against Chapin out at the Fielder's place. This white-eye girl sure had got Bob's balls in a knot.

Somebody went by the window. Jack Drago came in. The look on his long, pock-marked face gave warning that he was in one of his worst moods, but he asked, 'Who's that out there, that's got all them flies to hisself?'

Sanchez shrugged. When it became plain that Joseph Small Bear was not about to say anything, Chapin said, 'Some cow nurse. Got Joseph all riled up.'

Drago glanced at the Indian, yet knowing that he would probably be wasting his time waiting for an explanation. Chapin slopped rye into a shot-glass and handed it to Drago. Drago threw it back all-in-a-go and Chapin refilled the glass.

Less cautious than most, Drago asked Chapin outright, 'Yuh been out there? To Fielders'?'

'I been.' It required no elaboration. Drago, as were the others, was aware that Chapin, clearly having been rejected, was now in limbo, no doubt consumed by anger and humiliation, not knowing what to do next. But Chapin had a question of his own.

'Yuh seen Rosie?'

Drago's pocked face flushed. 'Rosie's vamoosed.' So that was it. Likely he had been taking it out on some of the other whores. Rosie's apparent defection, however, was by no means all of it, but that did not become clear immediately.

For the moment, though, their attention was diverted by Sanchez producing from one of his pockets a pack of greasy pasteboards. Chapin himself was not keen to play, but Joseph

Small Bear nodded and dragged forward a small, stained table. They would have to go find more chairs. Finally Chapin shrugged and that was the signal for Jack Drago, too, to nod his willingness to play. Maybe Chapin figured it would allow him some time to get his head straight about Sarah Fielder. A cold anger had been settling on him.

For an hour or so then, the four of them played a desultory game, Chapin, in the event, not able to concentrate properly and Jack Drago still deeply angry, presumably about what had become of Rosie Benato. There came a rattle at the door and a young, fresh-faced man came in. He was dressed in Levis and a grubby white shirt with no collar and had a pistol stuck in his waistband. This was Clem Cotton who had taken to following Bob Chapin around, watching him, fetching and carrying for him, seeking his approval; for Cotton clearly saw Chapin as a hard man who had attracted to himself these others who were of a like stripe. Somehow it made Cotton feel bigger — and older — just to be around them. There was one thing, however, that Cotton had taken good care to conceal from Bob Chapin, and that was that his own thoughts were never far from the pretty farm girl, Sarah Fielder. It burned him that Chapin was pursuing her so determinedly, but Cotton dare not show his own feelings. And like Chapin, the young man was well aware that the farm family would soon be gone and that it was therefore unlikely that he would ever see Sarah Fielder again. Not that Clem Cotton had ever had a real opportunity to get to know her. A few embarrassed words exchanged from time to time, and up to about a year ago, the occasional clumsy perfor-mance at a dance in Bethane. But mostly one of the freshly scrubbed shufflers and gawpers standing around the doorway.

Jack Drago now stood up and took a pace or two away from the table. Obviously he had lost patience with the card game. Chapin looked at Drago's back, then nodded to Clem Cotton. Cotton needed no second asking to take the vacated chair, his face flushed with pleasure. Chapin began shuffling the dirty cards. Again he glanced at Drago's back.

'She ain't worth gittin' all riled up about, Jack, that whore.'

Drago spat on the floor. After a moment or two, he said, 'Christ! It ain't the whore. She's pulled her pin an' gone, an' that's that. She kin go clear to Hell fer all I care. No, it ain't that. Some bastard's took that roan filly I brung down off'n Stoller's when he pulled out. I git my han's on whoever done it, then by God, I'll make the bastard pay.'

They knew that Drago had been much taken by the animal, so no wonder he had arrived in so foul a mood. Chapin knew that he would not

30

settle until he had found where the filly had got to.

So engrossed in the card game had Clem Cotton become that it was in an almost absent tone, and only after a long pause that he said, 'A roan filly? Reckon I seen one that was runnin' loose.'

Drago swivelled around. 'What's that, boy? When? Where?'

Startled by Drago's tone, Cotton lowered his cards to the table. 'When? 'Bout this time yesterday.'

'Where?'

As Drago took a pace towards him, Cotton's eyes shifted and he licked his lips. 'Out to the Fielder's farm, Jack.'

Now Chapin took a sharp interest, but he asked, 'Couldn't yuh see it was Jack's filly?'

Cotton looked confused, for he now had the unwanted attention of all of them. 'I ain't never seed that animal o' yourn, Jack.' Well, that was true. Cotton had not happened to be around just at the time that Drago had fetched it in, nor had Cotton visited, in recent times, the corral on what had been Chapin's ranch, where the filly had been temporarily installed. Cotton was a youngster who came and went, footloose, though putting in more frequent appearances now, wherever Chapin happened to be.

Jack Drago, punched one hand into the palm of the other. Then he started for the door. 'I'm goin' on out an' fetch that filly in.'

'Reckon I'll come along.' Chapin said. It might have seemed surprising in view of the fact that it would involve another visit to the Fielders' farm.

The others stood up, apparently ready to go with Drago, as well. Thus, by a small act, were set in motion the events that were to follow. But they all stopped and looked real hard at Clem Cotton when he added, 'Heeard some shootin' out that-aways, an' all.'

'What?' Chapin's tone was harsh.

'Out to Fielders'. Out that way,' Cotton said. 'Coupla shots.'

They all went out. The dead man, with his live flies, was still lying in the sandy alley.

3

The Fielder family was on the move. There were two wagons, one a heavy, canvas-covered vehicle drawn by a stolid four-horse team, the other, drawn by a pair, a much lighter rig and only partly covered. Ord Fielder was driving the larger wagon, while his brother-in-law, Henry Pedderson was up on the other. Hanni was on the seat next to her husband. Lilah, still shocked and occasionally tearful, was sitting close beside her mother. The wagon on which they were riding contained most of the household goods it was practical to carry away, and some articles had been lashed to the outside of the rig; lashed to a frame at the back was a large water-cask. Between the two wagons, Sarah Fielder was walking, while behind Henry Pedderson's rig came Lou Julius, bobbing along on the newly acquired roan filly, controlling it with reins and bridle but riding it bareback.

The stray animal, still somewhat wary of others, had come to Lou without hesitation, touching its nostrils to his outstretched hand, and thereafter had come willingly, nodding along at his heels wherever he went. Ord Fielder, observing, had known from the start that nothing could have persuaded the simple man to leave the roan behind, so he had shrugged and accepted that fact.

The wagon-horses and vehicles all happened to be Henry Pedderson's property, his contribution to the running of the farm, and were indeed, apart from the carbine, just about the sum total of Henry's goods and chattels.

Henry, wrapped in his own thoughts, was staring straight ahead, not unduly disturbed about quitting Bethane County after all this time or about the difficult journey that he knew lay before them all. But he was doing his best to shut out of his mind the demons that so often had tormented him through the years following the War Between the States. It might have been but yesterday when he had worn the Union blue, slogging his way along roads that seemed endless, often under burning sun or enduring rain that swept like a moving grey curtain across empty fields. Or crouching in inadequate cover, grasping hold of the earth itself, cowering beneath cannister and grapeshot, scything hot metal cutting comrades down like sickled grass. Not men, many of them. Boys for the most part, left bleeding and screaming, being roared at by the NCOs, Henry among those, trying hopelessly to rally them one more time, dreading the falling shot and dreading even more the long grey lines coming towards them, bayonets flashing.

Some terrible things had been done in the war, but many of them had been through fear and hunger. Advancing soldiers took whatever they could lay hands on; food, valuables, women. Foraging parties were always on the go, questing far and wide from the main column, sometimes taking dire chances. But all that was a part of the war. And Henry had seen more than one bunch of their own foragers lying in a ditch somewhere, shot to ribbons, caught by some of the local populace, cornered, a dozen miles from help. Comrades. Yet Henry and his kind had been no better, taking reprisals. There were times, dark times that it was best to thrust away from memory, when they had shot prisoners, boys in tattered grey, names unknown. All that Henry himself could ever recall about them, afterwards, when he had failed to brush recollection aside, was their eyes, wide and disbelieving, terrified, in the final moments of life. Now he shook his head as though to dislodge once again the images that refused to go away easily. Sometimes, only liquor would put them to flight; but that was only a temporary thing, anyway.

The wagon ahead of him was now moving more slowly because it was passing over some uneven ground, then dipping towards a dried-up creek on the banks of which stood clumps of cottonwood and walnut. Spiny brush had sprung up along the bed of the creek and there were numerous smooth grey stones. It reminded Henry of so many places in which he and others had taken cover from searching shellbursts. Ord's wagon, raked by arms of brush, went lurching across.

To Sarah, in a brown dress, walking ahead of him, Henry called, 'Watch your step crossin' the crick . . .'

She turned her head, her long black hair sliding across her narrow back, and nodded. She said nothing. Henry thought that she and Lilah walked as though their feet scarcely touched the ground. He cast a glance over his shoulder. The round-faced, round-headed Lou Julius, mounted on his prize, was tracking the wagon, a vague smile on his thick lips, a familiar straw hat with a wide brim set firmly in place, so firmly that it bent the tops of his ears over. The filly was moving kindly for Lou.

Henry's eyes swept left and right as his team came struggling up the opposite bank of the dead waterway. Ord would be keeping a lookout as well. They all had the nagging worry that the companions of the shot man might come when least expected, seeking retribution. Henry reckoned, though, that if they did come, it was more likely to be after sundown or just before sun-up. Ord did not own a rifle but Henry had given him, without high expectation of Ord's being able to use it effectively, a pistol, a Smith & Wesson Schofield. And of course, just behind him in the wagon, Henry was carrying the '66 Winchester carbine.

Now they were clear of what once had been a creek they were coming out onto a toe of land that had been an extremity of Bob Chapin's C-Bar ranch, a spread now fallen to ruin. *'Drunk hisself off'n it,'* had been the common opinion around Bethane County. Behind Chapin's back, of course, and well out of earshot.

Up ahead, Ord Fielder called out something that Henry could not hear. Sarah went trotting up level with her father on the leading wagon, then fell back again, looking at Henry and pointing ahead. There was a small structure of some kind. Eventually they came to it and stopped.

Its timbers grey with age, it was a ramshackle building, once a line shack of the C-Bar. To Ord and Hanni, it had seemed as good a place as any to haul up and maybe make some coffee and certainly break out some of the bread they had brought with them from the last bake at the farm.

★ ★ ★

Chapin, Jack Drago, Sanchez, Joseph Small Bear and young Clem Cotton were assembled out on what had been Chapin's ranch. They had arrived some minutes ago but had not dismounted. Come out to see if Jack Drago's filly had wandered back here or not. Well, the answer to that was plain enough. His mouth twisted, Drago nodded towards what remained of a corral.

'Pole come down. She walked right out.'

Walking their horses across the hardpack of the yard, near the abandoned ranch-house, a split-log structure with a low-pitched roof, they did swing down. Chapin shoved back his hat, then took a bottle from one of his saddle-bags and passed it around. When it got as far as Clem Cotton he near to choked on his swallow. There followed a good deal of walking around, belching and farting and passing the bottle from hand to hand. Just looking over what once had been all his, was enough to get Bob Chapin all riled up again, bringing it all back. Recent times had seen too many setbacks: beef prices; the failure of the railroad to come; the failure of the ranch; then Sarah Fielder. Chapin's companions left him with his own sombre thoughts. Yet had he but known it, Clem Cotton was remembering Sarah's face, too, and with a melancholy acceptance of hopelessness.

As though, by some odd prescience, Drago said, 'Fielders. Fielders is what yuh said, Clem.'

'Yeah.' Cotton was surprised and ashamed at the smallness of his own voice.

'Wa-al, I'm gonna git on over there an' take a look.'

Without discussing the matter further they all climbed back into saddles; but they were in no great rush and kept at the bottle until it was empty, and the last man to drink, Sanchez, flung it away.

After a little more than an hour they were walking their horses on to the hardpack of the homestead yard. There, they drew rein and looked around.

Chapin made a circling movement with one hand. They split up and rode slowly all around, peering into all the outbuildings, Joseph Small Bear riding inside the barn.

'Wagons,' Chapin called. 'They had two wagons on this place. An' a half-dozen horses. They was Pedderson's as I recall.' There were indeed wagon tracks to be seen, and horse apples, but not much else left here. That clear fact, however, did not deter Chapin from dismounting and wandering all through the house. Not all the furniture had been taken away. He reckoned he knew where Sarah (and probably Lilah) slept, and he spent several minutes standing looking around in the particular room. There were a couple of narrow cots but they had been stripped of all coverings. The empty drawers of a pine dresser were standing open. Chapin tarried a minute or two longer. He reckoned he could smell her scent. Then abruptly he turned and walked out.

Ord Fielder had risen from where he had been sitting, in bunch-grass, his back resting against one wall of the line shack.

'Time to git movin'.' Ord had been somewhat on edge all the while they had been resting here, for the two drifters had never been far from his mind. It was true that some 300 yards of back-trail was visible from where they were now, but on all other sides there was vegetation enough to conceal the approach of anyone who did not wish to be seen until the final few seconds.

They got up and went to the wagons, Sarah now choosing to ride on the second one alongside her Uncle Henry. Lou Julius unhitched the filly from the tailgate of that same wagon, and with surprising agility, slipped up and across her back.

Perhaps their brief unguardedness was because they were occupied with this, Lilah and Hanni putting uneaten provisions away. No fire had been lit to make coffee, for Ord had not wanted rising smoke to mark their presence here. Now, without warning, Jack Drago came walking out from brush behind the line shack, a pistol in his hand. To Henry Pedderson who, having laboriously got himself up on to the wagon-seat, would have reached for his carbine, Drago said, 'Do that, Henry, an' they'll have to take the other goddamn' leg off.' Henry, his face darkening, stopped moving. Lilah let out a scream. Hanni wrapped her arms around the girl. Ord was not carrying the Smith & Wesson and would not have tried to use it if he had been. He would have been no match for a man such as Drago, especially with a pistol already in hand. Lou Julius, his usually smiling face now showing his fear, was sitting on the roan, unmoving. He could not have had the slightest inkling of what had brought Jack Drago suddenly among them, armed, but any man holding a firearm was enough to strike terror into Lou.

To someone unseen, Drago shouted, 'C'mon in!' Not one but several men came walking out of the brush, leading horses, the last one to appear, Clem Cotton, leading Drago's horse as well as his own.

'Wa-al, I'll be damned,' Chapin said, 'here we all are ag'in.'

The farm family and the Chapin group stood staring for a time, then Drago asked, 'Where'd that moon-faced half-wit o' yourn git his han's on that roan filly?'

Lou, on the roan, seemed to shrink down as all eyes in the Chapin group became fixed on him. Ord Fielder spoke up.

'The filly, it come wanderin' on to the farm.' And he added, 'There ain't no brand on her.'

'Come wanderin' in,' said Drago slowly. 'Wa-al, sodbuster, I kin tell yuh 'xactly where it come wanderin' *from*, by God I can! Come wanderin' from where I left her, in a corral out on C-Bar, that's where. Some'dy bust her out o' there, mister. So we come to find out who.'

Henry Pedderson said, 'Nobody's been anywheres near C-Bar. Lou nor nobody.'

It was as though Henry had not spoken at all. Drago walked across the few yards separating him from the plump man on the roan. 'Git your ass down off'n my animal, half-wit.'

For the space of a few seconds Lou sat staring at Drago standing below him, Lou wanting to do as he had been told, yet incapable of doing it at once because his limbs simply refused to move.

Almost casually, Chapin called, 'Drag the shit-headed bastard off'n it, Jack.'

Drago had already made up his mind to do just that and now holstered the pistol. He shot out a muscular arm and seized Lou Julius's shirt, and with a savage tug, stepping back as he did it, hauled the round-faced man bodily off the horse and brought him thumping down into the bunch-grass. The boy-man's straw hat went spinning away. Startled, the filly went skitter-stepping to one side. Drago released his hold on Lou Julius, stepped over him and hastened to catch the loose reins and get the filly under control.

If by this time Henry Pedderson had again entertained some notion of lifting the carbine from behind him, it was rendered stillborn, for Ramon Sanchez had now drawn a pistol and was walking back and forth near the two wagons as though inviting either Henry or Ord Fielder to make some stupid move. Joseph Small Bear, arms folded, stood observing, saying nothing. Clem Cotton, with the two horses, had eyes only for Sarah Fielder, on Henry's wagon. The look that she gave him in return could have meant anything. Cotton thought it was a look of deep reproach, as though she could not believe that he could be a part of what was going on here. Hanni, on the other wagon, still had her arms wrapped firmly around Lilah and had heard Lou cry out when he had been dragged off the horse but had not seen it for it had happened behind where she was sitting. Lou lay where he had fallen, not hurt much but afraid to move. Drago had hitched the filly to the tailgate of Henry's wagon and now brought his full attention back to Lou.

Alarmed, Sarah said, 'Don't touch him! Leave him!'

Drago did not even glance at her. To Lou, he said, 'Yuh ain't that half-witted yuh cain't steal another man's horse.'

Henry said, 'Jack, he didn't steal your goddamn' horse. It come in jes' like Ord said.'

Drago looked at Henry. 'Don't git mouthy, Henry. It ain't nohow wise.'

Lou now took what he must have seen in his fuddled perception as a chance to get away from the terrifying Drago and suddenly went scrambling away on all fours. It was quite hopeless of course, and drew only laughter, Chapin standing with fists on his hips, watching. Now the very frightened Lou had come to his feet and, trying to hide from them, ran some forty feet and went inside the old line shack.

With Sanchez keeping half his attention on the wagon people and Clem Cotton off to one side, Joseph Small Bear, Bob Chapin and Drago faced towards the shack. Chapin called, 'C'mon out o' there, boy, or we'll sure come in after yuh!'

It had no effect beyond producing a whimpering sound from Lou Julius, inside. Then the rickety door was slammed shut.

Drago said, 'Now that was a real bad mistake.' He raised his voice. 'Come out, half-wit, or git smoked out!'

Joseph Small Bear grinned and Drago nodded to him. It was all that was needed. The Indian walked away and very soon returned with an armful of dry brush. When the Fielders realized what was about to happen there was a rush of raised voices. Henry Pedderson made as though to get down off his rig but Sanchez extended his pistol arm and shook his head.

Joseph Small Bear flung down the brush against the line shack, took a vesta from a pocket, struck it on a dry board and set the brush alight. At once flames started hungrily. The Indian stepped back. Chapin was still calling on Lou Julius to come out, now promising that he was about to be fried, but maybe the hapless Julius did not yet know what was happening for there was no response.

The flames came roaring up and now the tinder-dry boards caught hold. Ord Fielder was now shouting for Lou to get out quickly, but the door of the shack remained shut. Perhaps the man in there was huddled down in a corner, head buried in his arms, for there were no sounds, or at least none that could be heard above the roaring of the fire.

But suddenly the man inside the

shack must have known that something was badly wrong for he started up a high-pitched yelling. He got as far as the door and flung it open but he was faced with a swirl of smoke thick enough to screen him from view. When the smoke dissipated slightly, however, his outline could be seen, as though he was trying to get through the doorway and escape. But Sanchez half turned and fired his pistol, the lead hammering into a blackening doorpost. It was enough to drive the wild-eyed Julius back out of sight again. Sanchez brought his attention back to those on the wagons.

As the fire took greater hold, smoke climbing away, horses became restive. Bob Chapin had to go help Cotton contain them and lead them further off. Sanchez, though, would not allow the wagons to be shifted, and even with brakes hard on, there was some sturdy jerking and tugging by the head-bobbing teams. Joseph Small Bear went backing off from the blaze for waves of heat were coming off the fire, and now Lou Julius could plainly be heard, shrieking.

Ord Fielder yelled, 'Bob, fer God's sake!'

But Chapin took no heed. Indeed nobody, even those who wanted to, could have got anywhere near what had now become an inferno. The females were screaming and in tears.

Then they were all confronted by a nightmare sight. Heedless of pistols or of frightening men, Lou Julius, burning, came bursting from the flame-wreathed doorway of the shack, all of him ablaze, clothing and hair alike. Blindly, screaming in his agony, he ran towards Joseph Small Bear. At the last moment the Indian slipped aside and Lou Julius went plunging on, crashing in among brush that tore at him, setting the brush alight, until finally he fell, soundless, and became the heart of the fire in the brush, unrecognizable now as a human being.

4

Though not moving quickly, Alyard was riding towards where the smoke had been climbing strongly into the sky. It was still going up, but by now only in thin threads. Earlier, he had thought his ear had caught, faintly, the sound of a shot. Not a rifle shot. Only one, and just after the first of the smoke had shown itself in the north-east. It had added further unknown apprehensions to an already unquiet mind.

Certain links of chance had brought Alyard to this country. Then unexpected elements had confronted him, these sufficient to divert him, compel him towards further consideration of what he might do. His purpose remained clear. How he might go about his next move demanded careful thought. Sighting the smoke had brought him back to the present, and the implications disturbed him. He weaved the horse in and out among brush and scrub oak.

The Fielders had buried what remained of Lou Julius, these the most pitiful of remnants, and the family was still appalled by the sight and sound of his death. They were moving around the wagons in an almost bemused state. Bob Chapin and the oher men had gone, taking with them Jack Drago's roan filly. Drago, Ramon Sanchez and Joseph Small Bear had ridden away quickly with scarcely a glance at the Fielders, and in silence. It had seemed, though, that in the finish, Chapin had been ready to say something, maybe even make some statement of contrition, but finally he had found no words. And Clem Cotton, his youthful face ravaged by fear and guilt, had turned one last despairing look towards Sarah Fielder as though pleading for forgiveness, before following Chapin. It had all happened in such a short span of time and in such a fury of passion that even the Chapin party wanted to be shut of the place where it had happened.

In other circumstances, one of them might have thought to deprive Henry Pedderson of his dangerous carbine. Watching their backs as they had gone bobbing away, Henry had glanced towards his wagon, where the carbine was, but Ord Fielder had noticed, and said, 'Nope, Henry. Ain't our way. Ain't never been.'

Pedderson, arm hooked over his crutch, had flashed Ord a resentful look but had refrained from asking, '*So what is our way? Take whatever's shoved at us an' go crawlin' away to lick the wounds?*' Now Pedderson's head was aching dully and so was his left leg, feeling as sometimes it did, that the foot was still there. What had happened to it was years ago, but terrible images were still there, lying in wait to come springing without warning into Henry's mind. Recurrent, vivid images of men clawing at riven earth under bursting shot and raked by musketry, horses rearing and screaming, and with enemy horsemen to-ing and fro-ing in the mist along the river bottoms. Other memories, even worse. Some of them shameful enough to be thrust aside.

Henry stood staring at the still-smouldering patch of brush, tendrils of smoke still rising from it. The Fielders were about ready to move again, but in an odd way, seemed reluctant to do so. It was as though the spirit had been squeezed out of them, even Ord apparently drained of the will to say the word to move.

There was a sound. Another. The clinking of a bit-chain. Alyard came. On his crutch, Henry went swinging across to his wagon where the carbine lay, but at once Ord was shaken out of his do-nothing brooding.

'Nope, Henry!'

Pedderson stopped and for the second time gave his brother-in-law a most bleak glance. Then he shifted his attention back to Alyard. Black-clad man on a black horse. Something wrong about this bastard. Still here, nearby. Still hanging around. Come to the smoke, no doubt.

Alyard walked the horse closer, nodded to Ord Fielder, touched the wide brim of his hat with gloved fingers, presumably in deference to the Fielder females. He did not appear to look at any one of them in particular, but he had noticed where Sarah was and that she in turn was observing him from under her long lashes. The stench of the fire was all about in the air and what once had been a C-Bar line shack was now nothing more than a smouldering mess of charred lumber.

In a flat, spiritless tone, Ord Fielder told Alyard what had taken place here. He, too, might have questioned Alyard's still being in the vicinity, but chose not to. Henry Pedderson showed no such inhibitions, coming forward, swinging easily along on the crutch.

'Never thought to set eyes on yuh no more, mister.'

The dark, sunken gaze was turned on

Pedderson. With a flappy sound the black horse was shaking its head. 'It's open country, far as I can see,' Alyard said in his faintly Southern way.

Sizing him up afresh, Pedderson perhaps felt the same sensation that he had felt earlier, when Alyard had been at the farm, that he was looking at a man who had once been a Johnny Reb. Even thinking of the term always knotted Henry's belly. Unmoving, Alyard's eyes glittered. Ugly bastard, Henry thought, the horseshoe of a black moustache, the sharply planed face and the bluish, shaven jaw. Something not quite right about the man, so Henry's inner voice kept telling him.

Alyard swung a long leg over the cantle, getting down. Ord regarded him with interest, him and his equipment, eyes pausing briefly on the left-worn, butt-foremost pistol and, scabbarded on the horse, what was probably a Winchester repeater.

As though reading what was in Ord's

mind, Alyard, standing at the head of the black, asked, 'How far d'you reckon to travel? Which direction?'

'Travis County,' Ord said. 'Thereabouts.' He did not say how far that was, and when Alyard did not press the point, thought that either he had a pretty good idea or he didn't want to question Ord too closely.

Alyard asked, instead, 'The men who did this, they've gone for good?'

That had been in Ord's mind, too, and though he might not have wanted to say it within the hearing of the women, now had no option.

'Dunno that fer sure.' Because Bob Chapin was unpredictable, the more so when he had been at the bottle, as clearly he had recently. And Sanchez and Drago and the Indian were indeed very bad men. Frightening. Ord had three females to think about constantly. So in spite of the fact that Henry Pedderson wouldn't like it, he said, 'If'n yuh're headed the same way, Alyard, we'd be glad of your company.'

Apparently thankful, Hanni looked and nodded. As Ord thought he would, Henry had something to say.

'We don't know nothin' about this feller.'

Ord said, 'What we do know is Bob Chapin and them other vermin burned Lou. Half drunk an' lookin' fer an excuse to kill somethin'. Chapin, he couldn't stop that Injun doin' nothin' even if he'd a mind to. An' I reckon they ain't gone far.'

Henry was obdurate. 'We ain't got enough vittles.'

Alyard waited, not wanting to come into it.

Ord said, 'There's enough. We kin manage. An' there's trappin' we kin do'.

'Not once we're out on Deadman's,' Henry said. 'There ain't a lot that lives out there, far as I know. An' we'll need more water if this feller comes'.

The Fielder girls were watching and listening, Lilah looking openly wide-eyed at Alyard, Sarah apparently doing her best to avoid his eye but flicking a look from time to time. Alyard had caught every such glance without appearing to have done so. His whole attention seemed to be fixed on Henry Pedderson. Unsettlingly so.

Ord took the bull by the horns. He said to Alyard, 'Like I said, if you've a mind, ride along.'

Henry spun away, almost losing his balance, but he recovered quickly and went swinging across to his wagon. He flung the crutch in, noisily, then hauled himself up on to the seat. Ord, Hanni and Lilah climbed aboard the other wagon. Sarah chose to walk and it happened that, as Alyard turned the black horse around, she was alongside him. Henry's wagon was not set in motion right off, the driver sitting glaring at the back of the black-clad horseman and watching the easy-walking Sarah, her light brown skirts brushing seed-heads of grass.

For some little while, Sarah made no attempt to converse with the rider. No doubt she was still suffering badly the effects of what had happened to poor Lou Julius. It had been a horrifying episode and had indeed damaged the spirit of this farm family, coming atop of their having to abandon their land and their home. The father, Ord, though putting a resolute face to it all, must surely have reached the very depths of despair. Just for a moment or two, when Alyard had been talking with him, it had seemed that the dark rider's stare had softened somewhat, as though he might have recognized in Ord Fielder some quality to which he had warmed. By the time Alyard's attention had turned to Henry Pedderson there had been not the slightest trace of warmth. Certainly there had been no softening of eye.

As time passed, Henry Pedderson, some thirty yards behind, began noticing that Sarah was exchanging words with Alyard. Not by any means was it an animated conversation. It was sporadic, the girl, her long dark hair moving in the slight breeze, from time to time glancing up at the horseman. Now Henry wished he was close enough to hear what was being said. Yet he refrained from closing up behind them, lest his purpose became obvious.

In response to his short, laconic questions, Sarah had in fact imparted to Alyard the story, as she knew it, of Lou Julius, how he had been taken in by her ma and pa when Lou's own mother had died, the boy's father long gone, no one knew where. What circumstances had brought the elder Fielders into that situation Sarah did not say. Maybe she did not know.

Alyard received such information as had been given him without comment or probing questions. What he did say was, 'Your uncle, back there, he's taken this real hard.'

She said, 'He's got that carbine in the wagon. Maybe he'd have tried to get it. My pa thought so an' stopped him.' Her voice was honey-smooth. Alyard enjoyed the sound of it. He had been glancing briefly at her as she walked alongside him, storing up glimpses of her profile, her small, straight nose and her full lips, her faintly tanned face under a wide-brimmed straw hat that had a band of colourful cotton material, the tail of which was hanging down at the back. Her very dark hair, pulled back to expose small, flat ears, hung thickly almost to her buttocks.

If Alyard had been pleasantly impressed by her voice, Sarah Fielder had been surprised by the gentle tone of Alyard's. During the few words he had exchanged with Henry the black-clad man's voice had been almost harsh. The girl was puzzled by this man. At first, when he had come to the farm, she had felt not far short of afraid of him. The very look of him. The blackness of his clothing. Of the horse he rode. If ever she had imagined a manifestation of the devil himself, then maybe the image that would have come to her mind would have been something resembling Alyard.

The wagon ahead of them first

slowed, then rocked left and right as it began crossing an area of flinty rocks on hard, barren ground, the way forward bordered by dangerous thorn-brush. Alyard said nothing but extended his left arm towards Sarah. She took the gloved hand in both of hers. Effortlessly, Alyard hauled her up and she slid a leg across the horse and settled in behind the cantle, her knees pushed against the tied bedroll. She grasped the back of Alyard's belt with one hand, pulling her hat down more firmly with the other.

Henry Pedderson's eyes were little more than slits, watching Sarah slip so easily up on to Alyard's horse. The man on the black, while not turning his head, said to the girl, 'Henry, he'll not take kindly to this.'

Perhaps she was surprised to hear herself saying, 'There's a whole lot that Uncle Henry doesn't take kindly to.' Then, as though to let the man down more lightly, 'But he's been through some real bad times.'

'You mean in the war?'

'Yes.'

'The war was a time back.'

'To Uncle Henry it was no more'n yesterday. Sometimes he gets real down. Ma says he's gettin' worse.'

'Because of what happened to him? His foot?'

'Yes. That an' some other things my pa says we don't even know about.'

Alyard now gave his entire attention to guiding the black horse across this rough, difficult terrain, to emerge by and by on to an upslope where the footing was easier. Now, because the progress of Ord's wagon had been laborious, those on the horse were almost level with the wagon-team. Ord glanced across, and Hanni and the other girl. Seeing Sarah on Alyard's horse surprised them. Sarah appeared to be giving her whole attention to staying on the horse, clutching the cantle as well as Alyard. Henry's wagon had closed up somewhat but neither Sarah nor Alyard looked around.

Hanni Fielder, staring across at the pair on the horse, was not at all sure what to make of Alyard. Courteous towards her in a studied way, there was about him, also, a sense that was unsettling, almost of menace. True, at the farm they had shown him hospitality, but it was no more than they had done for other itinerants, even in the face of their own poor situation. They had not expected to set eyes on him again. Now, looking at her elder daughter sitting up behind this man gave Hanni a strange feeling and it was not altogether a pleasant one; as though someone had reached into the heart of her little family and had taken possession of something treasured.

The prospect now before them was of broken country, a place of brush and pines and scrub oak and hawthorn and a few cottonwoods. Here and there they would traverse relatively open spaces of bunch-grass, and it was in one of these clearings that Ord Fielder drew his wagon to a halt. All three on it got down. Alyard stopped. Sarah slipped down lightly off the horse. Alyard dismounted and led the black to the rear of Ord's wagon and hitched it there. Fifty feet behind, Henry's wagon stopped. Ord went to it with the slow, easy gait of the long-time sodbuster and stood exchanging a word or two with the man on the wagon-seat. All three females had gone off among the brush, out of sight.

It became plain to Alyard that Ord and Henry were engaged in a low-voiced argument, and the black-clad man was in no two minds over what it would be about. He did not need to look closely to know that Henry's burning eyes were fastened on him as he stood rubbing the black's warm nose. Then Henry said something that drew a sharp response from Ord Fielder. It was clear to Alyard that Henry, who must have been brooding deeply over it, wanted to turn and go back the way they had come; in fact far enough to find Jack Drago and square

69

matters for the dreadful death of Lou Julius. ' . . . can't let it lie, Ord . . . turn tail this way . . . ' No great champion for Lou, in life, maybe Henry thought that his manhood had been challenged by not doing more for the simple man when it was needed most.

Ord would have none of it. Even as the females were emerging from the brush he was saying, 'miles of this, then there's Deadman's Flats . . . out there, we got to keep movin' . . . one water hole . . . '

While the women were still out of earshot, Alyard came away from the hitched horse and walked towards the Pedderson wagon. He did not look up at Henry but, stopping in front of Ord, said, 'For what it's worth, there's been somebody along out backtrail this past hour. Just hangin' back, keepin' the wagons in sight.'

Now Henry, grunting, did get down and leaned against one of the front wheels. They stared back the way they had come, but there was a lot of vegetation, much of the country obscured. Henry looked very angry but probably it was with Alyard as much as anything.

Hanni, coming nearer, asked what the matter was. Ord told her. She stood staring from beneath her bonnet, down the back trail, a tendril of dark hair trembling against her forehead. Perhaps she was thinking, like Ord, that the two ragged drifters, having lost their companion to Henry's carbine, were now watching and waiting their chance for a shot at somebody.

5

In a clearing amid scrub oak and brush, they had come to a halt, some still mounted, others down out of saddles, flexing muscles. Bob Chapin reached a partly consumed bottle from a saddle-bag and took a strong swig, Adam's apple working. He belched loudly and handed the bottle to Jack Drago. To no one in particular, Chapin repeated what he had been saying all along, since the fire. 'Shoulda brung her along, after.' It was true that in a confused scene he had allowed a prime opportunity to go by and was now much regretting it. For it no longer mattered what Ord Fielder or his woman or Henry Pedderson might think. Not after the burning of the half-wit.

Drago was thoughtful. Then, passing the bottle up to Ramon Sanchez who was still sitting his horse, said, 'I'll go along, then, Bob. Reckon these here boys feel the same. There's other tidbits to be had. Ord Fielder's woman and the other, younger female.'

Chapin must have known that eventually it would come to this. The other females in the wagon-party would be the price that would be expected. Sanchez, the bottle part-way to his mouth, was looking at Chapin; and Drago and Joseph Small Bear. So, too, was Clem Cotton, standing at the head of his horse; but his face was drained of colour.

'So be it,' Chapin said. 'I git the older girl. You boys take what's left.'

Sanchez now took his swig before handing the bottle to Joseph Small Bear.

Drago said, 'Henry's got that god-damn' carbine. It was a bad mistake not takin' it.'

Chapin nodded slowly.

Sanchez, his small eyes still fixed on Chapin, said, '*Hombre* on black *cayuse*. Got rifle.' From a distance, that much had been observed. The presence of this man had puzzled them. Come out of nowhere. If he stayed, as looked likely, it doubled the Fielders' firepower. How good he might be they had no way of knowing, but Chapin, for one, did not care for unknown factors.

'Gotta git it done in a clean hit,' Drago said.

That was of some concern to Chapin, too. Things that might sound simple seldom turned out to be. And he was beginning to get the feeling that he was no longer in control here. If ever he had been, since the C-Bar turned belly-up.

* * *

Sarah Fielder was now riding on her father's wagon, whether by choice or because something had been said to her Alyard did not know. She was sitting in behind her pa and ma and Lilah, no hat on, her black hair falling freely around her narrow shoulders and down her back.

Gradually Alyard had fallen in behind the second wagon and was turning his head frequently to observe as much as he could of their backtrail. Since he had spoken about others being in the vicinity and, as he believed, tracking the wagons, the farm group had fallen quiet, even Henry. But earlier, on the quiet, Henry had left Ord Fielder in no doubt as to his opinion.

'This Alyard, he could be one on 'em. Come walkin' in out o' God knows where. Rid off an' then it turns out he didn't go nowheres.'

Ord had given this view some thought but had given no indication of whether he even entertained the notion or not. His elder girl's attitude had puzzled Ord. Right from her earliest days Sarah had shown a marked disinclination to take readily to strangers. Men in particular. But there was no doubt that Henry didn't cotton to this Alyard. And a blind man could see that the feeling was mutual.

As the day wore on, through the brief

halts for food, Alyard had become more sensitive to the atmosphere of tension. Seemingly lost in his own thoughts (for Henry, at least, had from time to time craned around to see exactly where the horseman was) he was nonetheless alert, dark eyes probing this way and that, seeking any sign of dust, any rise of birds which would indicate the presence of horsemen in the vicinity. That so far there had been nothing to see had by no means assuaged Alyard's misgivings. Mile after mile of uneventful progress could promote among travellers feelings of somnolence and, in the present circumstance, a fatal vulnerability. Alyard wondered if Henry Pedderson accepted what he had said, or whether his antipathy towards Alyard would have the effect of making him lose the edge of alertness. Now Alyard himself had to shake free of thoughts of the one-footed man on the wagon just ahead, but remembering what Sarah had said, of Pedderson and the war. Sergeant in the infantry. Henry had had a real bad war, according to Sarah.

Some last-second sense of present danger probably saved him. Alyard checked the stride of the lean black. The waft of the bullet seemed to come almost before the lashing of the rifle 'way across to Alyard's right, in deep brush. The horse reared as its rider, kicking free of the stirrups, left the saddle and went plunging into thick bunch-grass. The black went swiftly skipping away, shaking its head and whickering.

There was a flurry of activity at the wagons, both of which had been stopped and braked. People were tumbling out and seeking shelter beneath the rigs, Henry Pedderson not slow to react, taking with him the carbine. Alyard's rifle was still in its scabbard, on the horse. The black, having skittered away for a few yards, had stopped and was now standing with its head up and ears pricked, looking towards some thorn brush about forty yards away.

Shaken by his plunge to the ground, Alyard now rolled on his right side, unthonged the hammer and drew the pistol, a blue-black Frontier Colt .44, and cocked it. Now he followed the stare of the horse. Nothing to be seen, yet the black was clearly aware of the presence of other animals. Alyard was lying flat as he could, holding the Frontier in his stretched-out, gloved right hand.

Nobody showed. Maybe they could not see Henry Pedderson clearly and were leery of his carbine. He had become known for fancying the weapon. When it seemed, after a long silence, that nothing more was going to happen, a voice was raised, and it was the voice of a man who had been at the bottle. Bob Chapin.

'Ord? Ord Fielder?'

'I kin hear yuh, Bob. What is it yuh want? What dang fool shot that there rifle off?'

There was a longish pause before Chapin answered. 'Didn't reckon to hit nobody, Ord.' Lying in the grass some distance away, Alyard well knew that was a lie. The close waft of the bullet had told him that it had been meant to drop him. 'An' it ain't what I want, Ord, it's who. Yuh know why I come, afore. Wa-al, I've come ag'in, an' I don't reckon to parley a lot over a sodbuster's li'l fe-male. Not nohow. I want her, Ord, an' by God, I mean to have her.'

Before Ord could say anything, Hanni did, unable to contain her anger.

'Yuh'll keep well clear o' my girl, Bob! Yuh was told afore, real plain! She'll not have yuh, now or any time!'

Again there was a silence. It ran on for what must have been a minute. Then Chapin called, 'Ain't got no quarrel with yuh, neither on yuh. We been neighbours a good long while. Dunno where yuh're headed an' I reckon it don't matter. Yuh kin git on yuh're way, you, Hanni an' the young 'un. It's easy done, Ord, an' no more trouble.'

Ord did not delay in answering that.

'Bob, yuh heeard what Hanni said. Wastin' time with all this carry-on. We're headin' on down to Travis County. We've all on us set out, an' all on us is gonna git there. Now why don't yuh pull back from this here nonsense an' 'llow peaceable folks go in peace? Yuh done enough harm already, Bob, you an' that scum yuh got with yuh. There warn't no call to harm Lou. He never did no harm to nobody an' he warn't no hossthief. It was a terrible thing, Bob, an yuh coulda stopped it.'

Chapin shouted right back, no doubt because all the raw spots had been rubbed. 'Yuh're commencin' to rile me real bad, Ord!' Other voices were carrying to those at the wagons, some kind of ragged argument going on, but what was being said could not be distinguished. Then without warning another shot came lashing and lead whacked through the canvas of the wagon, near the top of the canopy. Henry's carbine blasted. Shooting on the blind though, Henry

80

was. Alyard did not shoot.

It was Bob Chapin who called next. 'Hold up! Hold up!' Maybe it had been someone else in his party who had fired the shot, and that had been what the argument had been about. Even if it had all been under Chapin's control, perhaps it was slipping away fast. Then, surprisingly, Chapin called to Alyard.

'Feller on the black . . . dunno who yuh be, mister, but I'll say this: I'll give yuh one chance to git on that hoss there an' ride on out. An' no harm done, it ain't your argyment.'

Alyard waited for a few seconds to tick by before calling, 'I come an' I go where an' when I please, mister. Right now, here's where I am an' here's where I'll stay.'

It drew no reponse. Alyard could just see Henry's face under the wagon, turned in his direction. There was no approval to be read in it. All fell quiet again. Time was passing. The afternoon was wearing on. Flies were whirling and settling on bare skin and being wafted away. Alyard's horse, wandering further off, reins trailing, was now quite settled.

Surprisingly, Clem Cotton's voice was the next to be heard.

'Mr Fielder?'

'That you, Clem?'

'Yeah, it's me . . . Mr Fielder, will yuh have them fellers there hold fire so I kin come on in?'

'Come in? What fer?'

'Talk, Mr Fielder. I got some things that's got to be said.'

First Ord glanced at Hanni, then said, 'Henry . . . Mr Alyard . . . Clem's gonna come in.' Then he raised his voice some more. 'I told 'em, Clem!'

Presently there was a stirring among the nearest of the brush, and Clem Cotton, up on his sorrel horse, appeared, walking the animal into the clear, approaching the wagons across the stretch of bunch-grass. Cotton was pale and appeared to be very tense, as though an unexpected sound would be all that was needed to spook him. When he was about ten yards from the Fielder wagon, all the set faces beneath it staring at him, he drew the sorrel to a halt and got down out of the saddle. More than ever he looked like a shiftless boy who has got clear out of his depth.

'What's it about, Clem?' Ord had the Smith & Wesson Schofield pistol in his hand but gave every impression of being uncomfortable with it.

Cotton swallowed hard and led the horse forward and tied it to the wagon.

'There's things he wants said, Bob, that is. He reckoned he warn't gonna git nowheres like it was. That's why he sent me.' Cotton's weak eyes kept flicking to Sarah.

Ord asked, 'Them other fellers, they all with Bob still?'

Cotton nodded jerkily. 'All three.'

'Drago, I know. An' I know who that Mex feller is: Ramon Sanchez. Who's the Indian?'

'That there's Joseph Small Bear.' Cotton licked dry lips. 'Mr Fielder, he's a real mean 'un.'

'They're all real mean, boy. They showed us already jes' how mean. I'm surprised to see yuh still hangin' 'round with men like that.'

Cotton's boyish face went scarlet. Again he licked his lips. 'I'd best say what I come — what Bob said fer me to say.'

'Mebbe yuh had.'

Cotton took a long, uneven breath. 'Bob said he sure means it, fer yuh to move on.'

'Without Sarah.'

Cotton found that he couldn't look at her any more. 'Yeah . . . ' Then, 'An' I come to . . . to take her back.' Hanni would have jumped in right there but Cotton hurried on. 'Right soon it's gonna be sundown.' His voice was much lower, the words tumbling out. 'They're lookin' to take . . . ' He was having real trouble now. 'Soon as they git aholt o' Sarah, they're lookin' to . . . to take Lilah an' Miz Fielder an' all. Bob, he's been kinda argyfyin' over that, but he cain't do nothin' no more.

They'll not shift.'

Softly, Hanni said, 'Dear God!' Lilah made a whimpering noise and clung to her mother. Sarah spoke up, staring at Clem Cotton, willing him to look at her.

'An' you're one of 'em, Clem. One o' these . . . animals!'

Violently the boy shook his head. 'No! No I ain't!' To Ord, hissing the words, he said, 'Let me stay, Mr Fielder. I got this here.' He touched the handle of a pistol that was pushed down in his waistband.

Hanni said, 'Ord, we can't trust him.'

Henry, calling softly from beneath his wagon, asked, 'What's all the whisperin about?'

'Crawl across,' Ord said. 'Reckon they'll not let fly while he's still talkin'.'

Presently Henry, dragging the crutch and with his carbine, came to them and Ord told him what was what. Henry's reaction was to point the carbine at Clem Cotton.

'If they do shoot,' Henry said, 'this

little bastard, he'll go real early.'

'If he stays,' Ord said doggedly, 'we got one more pistol.'

'Wa-al,' said Henry, 'there ain't no way he's gonna git behind *me* with it.'

They had not noticed that Alyard had been on the move. They were startled when they heard his voice from only a few yards away.

'Ord, back there a'ways there's some low ground. Maybe Miz Fielder an' your daughters ought to go there for better cover.'

To Hanni, Ord said quietly. 'It'd make sense to do like Mr Alyard says.'

Hanni did not argue but spoke briefly to the girls, then all three went crawling away through the long grass. One by one they passed the dark, hard-faced Alyard lying, pistol in hand, scarcely visible from only a few feet away. Hanni was first to find what he had been talking about, a low, trench-like depression in the ground. Lilah followed her mother. Sarah was last to pass Alyard and briefly touched his arm by way of thanks, then went crawling on to join her mother and her sister.

Clem Cotton, given the final word by Ord Fielder and a look of undisguised malevolence by Henry Pedderson, took a chance, unhitched the sorrel from the wagon and led it behind some nearby brush and tied it there, out of view.

It did not take Bob Chapin long to figure out what was going on. In what was nearly the last of the daylight, Chapin called to the youngster, 'Don't think I ain't figured out why yuh ain't come back, boy! Wa-al, that li'l lady, she ain't gonna be fer you, Clem. An' when yuh ain't no more use to One-Foot, he'll blow yore asshole through yore mouth! But that ain't the half o' what's gonna happen if'n I git a-holt o' yuh first!'

For the night hours, Henry took it upon himself to organize the disposition of all concerned. He would resume his place under the second wagon, Ord Fielder under his own vehicle, Alyard to Fielder's left and back some ten yards, to protect the women on that side from a loop-around by Chapin. Clem Cotton would be between the wagons, Henry saying, 'Where I kin keep an eye on him.' No food would be taken, and no water. They would wait out the hours of darkness. Chapin and his group had been at the bottle and no doubt they would go on drinking for as long as their supply lasted. They would be in no condition, Henry maintained, to approach the wagons without creating some kind of racket. Henry volunteered to stay awake and he advised the others to rest while they could.

Whoever else slept, even fitfully, was not clear, but when the first grey streaks of the new day were drawn across the eastern horizon, it did not take Henry Pedderson long to observe that Clem Cotton was not where he ought to have been. Nor was he to be found anywhere else in the vicinity of the wagons. The sorrel was still tied where Clem had left it. Either the boy had gone inching back across the relatively open space to rejoin Bob Chapin or they had come and got him. If they had done that, then probably they had sent Joseph Small Bear. Nothing had been seen or heard.

6

The early morning was windless. Cramped and with eyes burning from nervous sleep, the wagon people, coming slowly and carefully together, were challenged by the realization that at least one of Chapin's terrible companions had moved among them in the night. Yet now, though they were listening intently, they could hear no sounds of activity out there in the brush. And no voices. Only birdsong. Little by little they came to a sense that the Chapin party, for reasons unknown, had gone.

Ord would have approached the brush where they knew Chapin had been, but Hanni spoke strongly against it. Henry, though he could move expertly with the aid of the crutch, would be at a disadvantage until he could get into a firing position, propping his carbine. Alyard, however, did not need to be asked, or account for his movements. He left his Winchester, which he had retrieved during the night, drew the Frontier Colt and stood up. He walked away from the wagons across the deep bunch-grass towards the brush out of which Clem Cotton had come riding. All eyes were fastened on the long back of the black-clad man, but who soon enough passed from sight.

Alyard was advancing slowly, pistol extended, eyes probing left and right, from time to time glancing behind him. He came upon several areas where the grass had been trampled flat. In one place lay an empty rye bottle. Alyard figured they would be carrying more liquor. Further on, the earth had been cut up by horses and there were piles of horse apples. The area seemed to have been abandoned. Alyard, however, was not so easily satisfied. Taking his time and moving quietly, he set about making a complete circuit of the place where the farm wagons were standing. When he had completed it, he did not return immediately to the Fielders. From tracks he had found, indications were that Chapin and those with him had headed south-west. If they were to maintain that direction, then soon they would be out on the arid, brush-pocked Deadman's Flats. It was across that unappealing stretch of country that Ord Fielder intended taking his family. Bob Chapin along the backtrail or keeping some kind of intermittent watch from off to either side of them was one thing; Chapin somewhere out ahead was something else. Then there was the question of Clem Cotton's sorrel. Having come in and got hold of Cotton, it was a mystery to Alyard why they had not taken the horse as well. Maybe it had been purely on account of making too much noise.

Other matters were teasing his mind, demanding answers that he was now incapable of giving. Chance might have brought him to where he was now, but it had been a mixture of chance and of discreet enquiries that had brought him to this part of the country. Yet nothing, he thought, ever turned out to be as straightforward as might have been expected. Most often, the unexpected had to be dealt with. There might be hesitations, even agonies of mind to be endured. Was it this that separated him, Tom Alyard, from the Bob Chapins? The Alyard observed by others, the hard, unyielding man, would seem to give the lie to that. Yet could acts that he had committed in the past fall far short of acts committed by a man of Chapin's stripe? Considerations such as these, he found, and uncomfortably, were like thrusts from a fine blade.

There was nothing that he could not escape: Sarah Fielder, the look of her, her warm proximity up behind him on the horse, was gnawing at him. Was this so different from the way she had so completely captured the mind of Bob Chapin? Or what had captivated poor Clem Cotton? He found that he was still holding the pistol. He eased it back into its holster and thumbed the hammer-thong into place. He walked from the cover of the brush to where the wagons were. To Ord Fielder's raised eyebrows Alyard shook his head.

'Pulled out.' And he added, 'Southwest.' They would all know what that meant.

Nonetheless they now came out from beneath the wagon. All stood up, Henry too, leaning on his crutch. There was much stretching of legs and arms, and from the females a rush of talk, no doubt a nervous manifestation of relief that, for the time being at least, the dire threat to them had lifted. Soon, however, as the wagons went creaking on, the stark reality of their situation would return to plague them. Hanni even put to Ord the obvious alternative to their going on down to Travis County.

'We could jes' turn back.'

'Turn back to where? Up to Montrose? Salter's Ferry? Where? There ain't nothin' fer the likes of us up there, Hanni. At least, we're headin' to where we know there's kinfolks.' Well-established kinfolks, too. Doing real well, last time they'd heard. That was the lure.

Lilah asked outright, 'They really gone, Pa? Rid away an' not comin' back?'

Ord must have known that it would have been stupid to make pretences. 'We cain't know that, honey. We kin on'y hope. An' we'll be keepin' a right good look out. If they wasn't afeared o' the guns we got, they'd 've done harm to us afore this.'

Then Lilah asked the dark man, 'Yuh gonna stay, Mr Alyard? Yuh gonna ride along, all acrost them flats?'

Straight-faced, Alyard said, 'Turns out I'm headin' that way, Lilah. I'd be real glad o' the company.'

Sarah smiled. It was like the opening of a flower. Henry Pedderson, however, was not smiling, and Alyard bent upon the one-footed man a most enigmatic look, as though about to say something more, directed at Henry, but he held back, and instead gave Sarah the faintest of smiles. Hanni looked steadily at Alyard then turned away.

They set out, Sarah reverting to walking behind her pa's wagon, but this time Alyard was not riding beside her. He had chosen to go out ahead of the Fielders, rifle unscabbarded, the butt-plate resting on one knee. There was still a stretch of brush-clogged, tim-bered country to pass through before they would arrive at the edge of Deadman's Flats, and it was Alyard's hope to pick up the tracks left by the Chapin party. Yet he was alert to the possibility that at some place along the way, Chapin might simply lie in wait for the wagons, relying on surprise to overcome the threat of the wagoners' firearms and to have his companions seize the females.

From time to time, Alyard came upon sign which told him of the passing of the Chapin party, but none of his circling and scouting yielded any evidence of possible ambush. Half a day closer to Deadman's Flats, however, where brush and trees had begun to thin out, affording a longer view ahead, Alyard, now a hundred yards beyond the Fielder wagons, drew the black horse to a halt. The animal had already become disturbed by something in the vicinity, but at first Alyard had no idea what it was. Then he stiffened in the saddle and gripped the Winchester and levered a round into the chamber. The horse was moving under him restlessly, and Alyard sought by softvoiced reassurances, to quieten it.

Some fifty yards ahead, an object of some kind was suspended from a sturdy branch of a tree. Alyard nudged the head-tossing, reluctant horse forward, but after no more than ten yards, stopped it again. Now he could see what the object was.

Stripped of his upper clothing, Clem Cotton was hanging from the pine branch by what Alyard at first thought was the wrists. Then it became clear that the youngster had been strung up with leather thongs, not by the wrists, but by the thumbs. There were some red weals on his torso. His head was hanging loosely. Yet Alyard believed that Cotton was alive. Below his bootless, stockinged feet was a pile of dry brush.

Alyard did not approach the inertly suspended Cotton. Instead he turned the black and urged it in behind the shelter of some green brush. As soon as he was certain that he was well out of sight of those who, no doubt, were watching the hanging boy, Alyard called loudly, 'Ain't takin' the bait today, Bob!'

After a short interval, Chapin's voice, from a little distance away, called, 'Reckoned yuh'd be too fly, mister . . . but it was worth a try.' Clearly Chapin had made some assessment of Alyard, presumably based on his appearance and had concluded that he was the kind of man it would pay to tread around with some care. Part of the reason, perhaps, for Chapin's not having come in, bull-headed and whiskey-fired, at the Fielder wagons. And maybe why they had not tried to take Sarah when they had got Clem Cotton. That, and Henry's carbine. They must now regret not having lifted that when they had the chance.

Alyard dismounted and led the horse away, keeping as much as possible among brush until he saw the oncoming wagons. He stepped into view, holding the Winchester aloft. Ord brought his rig to a stop. Sarah came walking, swishing through the grass, and stopped alongside her pa's team, watching Alyard. Henry Pedderson's wagon was eventually pulled to a halt some ten yards behind Ord.

Bluntly Alyard told them what was up ahead. Ord was plainly taken aback.

'What in the name o' God are they up to?'

Henry said, 'Bob's a man that don't like bein' crossed. But what's been done to Clem, I'd put that down to that goddamn' redskin.'

Alyard gave Henry a long, unsmiling look, but to Ord, said, 'My advice is head away, yonder, put some distance between them an' us. I didn't clap eyes on any of 'em, but if I'd gone to Cotton I'd have been nailed for sure.'

Ord studied the terrain. If he did as Alyard had suggested, it would mean tough going, sturdy though the wagons were. And if they did angle away from their present line, their progress must be slowed. They would lose hours. And waiting for them, of course, were Deadman's Flats. The other factor was Henry, who now spoke up.

'My opinion, Ord, we head the way we're headed now.' Alyard knew that it was as much a challenge to the advice he had given Ord as anything else, Henry asserting himself as a member of this family, and as a man of some experience. Shrewd old soldier. Bluecoat, too, and one who'd had three stripes. And Henry must have known that Bob Chapin would never take him cheaply, no matter what might be said while exchanging insults. The one-footed man still commanded some respect.

In the finish, Ord said nothing directly to Alyard but when he made the arm-movement for them to start again, it was obvious that they were to continue in the direction in which they had been heading. Alyard's face was expressionless. He made no comment, having said all that he intended saying. But Chapin would be getting ready to make some play, of that they could be certain. In Alyard's view, continuing along this line would hand him his chance to make it.

One thing Ord did insist on was that Hanni, Sarah and Lilah all get inside the leading wagon, get down among the belongings and stay out of sight. And he made clear that he wanted Henry's wagon to track his own more closely. Without comment, Alyard, on the black and with rifle in hand, rode ahead, but this time by no more than ten yards.

They were moving slowly but soon

came within sight of the hapless Clem Cotton suspended from the pine branch. Being confronted with this sight maybe had a greater effect on Ord Fielder than he had imagined it would, for he swore softly, and though he had not intended to, drew the team to a stop. Cotton was conscious, something confirmed by a small movement of his head.

Surprisingly, Bob Chapin came walking into view. Not steady on his feet, he had several days' growth of whiskers, was looking very unkempt indeed and a little wild-eyed. Jack Drago appeared, too, rifle held across his chest. They were about forty yards ahead of the wagons and to the right, but were only a dozen feet from the suspended Clem Cotton. As usual, Chapin was wearing a pistol, but he had not drawn it. There could be no doubt that he had been at the bottle recently. Alyard wondered if it was now necessary for Chapin to keep personal demons at bay. Henry well knew the signs. He had dealt with demons probably much like them, in much the same fashion, in his time. Plainly no such phantoms were circling Jack Drago. His face was as expressionless, his eyes as fish-dead as no doubt would be those of the unseen Indian, or those of Sanchez. Chapin's first utterance, his voice thickened, was a question.

'Where's Clem's mount?'

It was Alyard who answered. 'I turned that sorrel loose. Left all the gear in the brush. Figured if I brought it along, some bastard might come lookin' an' make accusations an' want to burn my ass off.'

Chapin's yellow teeth showed in what could have started as a smile. He nodded. 'Ah, wa-al, it ain't o' no account no more. This double-crossin' li'l shit ain't gonna have no use fer it. Afore long, he'll be ridin' an anvil in Hell.'

Ord said, 'He's no more'n a boy, Bob. Why don't yuh cut 'im down, stop all this here carry-on?'

'I'm real touched, Ord,' said Chapin, 'fer all this concern fer the likes o' Clem who warn't o' no account at all, that I kin recall.'

Small whimpering noises had begun coming from the suspended Cotton and his head had begun wagging from side to side. Against all her husband's advice, Hanni Fielder now sat up and leaned an arm across the back of the wagon-seat.

'Bob, in the name of God take that boy down!'

In a mockery of deference Chapin touched the brim of his hat and bobbed his head.

'Miz Fielder. Figured yuh'd be in there somewheres. Reckon them two prairie flowers is all scrooched up there an' all. Wa-al, that's what we come about.' He was blinking his foxy eyes at Ord. 'Do yuh a deal, Ord. Right now. Flat on the barrel. Yuh gittin' all knotted up over this li'l bag o' shit I got hangin' here. So, here's the deal. Yuh kin have the boy. Cut the bastard down yore own self if yuh got a mind to. Take 'im along, wet thumbs an' all. All yuh got to do is set them ladies down, all three, an' yuh go rollin' on. You, One-Foot an' that there feller that come out o' nowheres, an' kin now git on back there.'

'Bob, yuh got to be *loco*!'

Chapin shrugged. 'Had me a few shots, through the day. *Loco*?' The man who had lost the C-Bar shook his head. 'Yuh done lost that patch o' dirt back there, Ord. Now yuh got some saddle-bum an' a cripple to help yuh go belly-up somewheres else. Time yuh shucked some o' yore freight.'

It seemed that Ord Fielder might reach into the wagon, presumably for the pistol, but Drago shifted the rifle. He did not point it at Ord, for Alyard's Winchester was being held so that a small shift would bring it to bear on either Drago or Chapin. Drago's movement, however, was quite enough to check the farmer.

Chapin said, 'Like I said, yuh got all

that concern fer this boy here, yuh'll do like I say. On the other hand, yuh kin jes' leave. If yuh do, yuh kin be sure these boys'll spend some time fryin' his ass off.' They saw now that Ramon Sanchez and Joseph Small Bear had come easing into view. 'Suit yorself, Ord,' Chapin said.

Ord said, 'Bluff, Bob.' But his voice said he was not at all sure. Nonetheless, he half turned his head, the better for Henry to hear him. 'Move 'em on!' Alyard, sitting the black, waited as the wagons went creaking by, Henry, when he came, seen to be sitting with his footless leg hooked firmly around the seat, long lines in one hand, the carbine in the other and looking as though he sure knew how to use it, one-handed.

Even so, Drago called, 'Four to two! Yuh wouldn't stand no chance!'

'Nor you, neither, Jack,' said Henry. 'First 'un down. This'n's got a kick like a drunken mule.'

The wagons were allowed to pass by unmolested and soon go beyond screening trees and brush. But when Alyard and Henry looked back they could see the brownish smoke already climbing above the treetops and they could hear the crackling of fire.

7

Henry Pedderson's progress across the lumpy bunch-grass, having to avoid the reach of sharply-spiked brush was something to see. Alyard, having dismounted, running in Henry's wake, observed it closely, as he had been observing all that Henry did, since first setting eyes on him. When Henry arrived at a place from which he could see what was happening, though it had not been difficult to work out, he stopped, propped on the crutch and laid the carbine across the top of it. Alyard came level with the one-footed man and stopped some four yards to the right of him.

The pile of brush beneath Clem Cotton had been lit. There was little smoke to be seen now, all fire, and roaring deeply, already almost enclosing the suspended man, his pants well alight as he bucked and swung, trying to climb upon the very air itself to escape, a flaring, screaming pendulum. Through the heat-haze could be seen the shimmering images of four men, Chapin, Drago, Sanchez and Joseph Small Bear. They had seen Alyard and Henry Pedderson come back. Chapin called out something but the roaring of the flames and the screaming of the wildly plunging Clem Cotton buried whatever it had been.

Henry, swearing softly, muttering, squinted along the short barrel of the carbine. When the weapon went off, all four who were standing beyond the burning man went diving to the ground at the instant that Cotton's skull, blazing with pinkish flame, exploded redly.

Even before anybody else quite realized what had happened, Pedderson and Alyard had quit the scene. Alyard had gone backing away, covering Henry's expert but nonetheless hazardous retreat. For good measure, Alyard, sighting carefully, let go a lashing shot, levered fast, the spent shell sent spinning, then fired again over the heads of the prone men. The body of Clem Cotton, now burned almost to a blackened husk, one of the leather thongs gave way, and what was left of Cotton was now hanging tenuously by one claw-like hand. There was an answering shot, this fired by Jack Drago, but it was not much more than a gesture, for by that time not only had Henry Pedderson departed, but Alyard as well.

Ord Fielder was down off his wagon, the Schofield pistol held awkwardly, waiting to see what was going to happen. Alyard could hear Henry saying urgently, 'Git back up, Ord! Git it rollin'! They'll make a try fer us!'

Alyard unhitched the black from the tailgate of Henry's wagon and swung up. While the two wagons were got under way, Alyard turned the horse so that he was facing their backtrail, waiting for Chapin, or any of them, to show a face. The black was side-stepping, its head tossing, unsettled by all the rushing around, the sudden movements and nearby gunfire. By the time that the first of the horsemen came into Alyard's view the wagons were thirty yards away. The riders coming were Sanchez and Joseph Small Bear. Alyard, levelling the Winchester, but in some difficulty because of the still restive horse, shot between them.

The effect was immediate, Sanchez veering one way, the Indian the other. Now Drago and Chapin had appeared but hauled up short, for the bullet must have passed very close to them. Sanchez was in trouble, having got too close to a bunch of thorn brush. Joseph Small Bear had slipped from sight altogether. Alyard shot again. Drago and Chapin turned their horses, sending them bounding away towards cover. It was plain that Alyard was regarded as a very dangerous type of man.

When Alyard was reasonably sure

that for the moment the pursuit had burned out, he turned the horse and went spurring away in the wake of the wagons. Yet, when he got to within a dozen yards of the one being driven by Henry, he reined in again and again turned the horse about. Nobody in sight. Alyard, however, did not call out to Henry or Ord at this point, preferring them to go on urging the teams on, to put distance between this place, where there was too much concealment for Alyard's liking, and the Chapin party.

After some ten minutes, though, Ord Fielder let up on his team and finally brought it to a halt. Henry hauled up about ten yards behind Ord. The next thing that happened was that Sarah Fielder climbed down off her pa's wagon and stood watching the loping black horse, with Alyard, come up to them and stop. Staring at Alyard, Sarah gave him a faint smile.

Henry asked, 'Any sign?'

Alyard shook his head.

Ord asked, 'That you shootin' back there?'

'It was,' said Alyard. 'I put a couple past their ears. It's checked 'em for now. I doubt that's the end of it.'

From there on they travelled at a lesser pace than they had started out. Alyard resumed riding drag. Both of the Fielder girls were walking along-side their pa's wagon, both frequently glancing back as though to reassure themselves that the dark-clad man was still coming.

During this time, Hanni Fielder became withdrawn and tense. Ord could not get much out of her and in the finish, gave up. She would come to herself in due time. For her and her family this had been a dreadful few days. They had severed connections with the farm, all the familiar, day-to-day things. There had been, too, occasional visits to the town, Bethane, and a few friends there, before the drift-away had started. Now, ahead of them, vegetation thinning out, lay the

113

shimmering, brush-dotted waste, the sweltering, dust-raked Deadman's Flats. Going easy, resting the animals, taking shade beneath the wagons in the worst of the sun's heat, conserving water, Ord had estimated that the flats would take them five days to cross. But once beyond them, skirting some barren hills, they would come to the Sligh River and the town of Doell's Ferry. From there, having rested and reprovisioned, they would traverse cattle lands and enter Travis County, their goal.

Not far out on the flats, gritty dust, gathered on a lift of hot wind, raked the people and the wagons and their teams. The Fielder girls climbed back in to get under the hooped canvas. Alyard, still regarding not only their backtrail but the brush-studded but otherwise featureless country lying ahead and on either hand, pulled up his blue bandanna so that only a narrow strip remained between it and his thonged-down hat. He was concerned that Chapin, should he choose to pursue them as far as this bleak place, might contrive to loop around them to lie in wait somewhere up ahead. This wind-moving dust might mask other dust, that made by hastening riders to the left or to the right.

How the tortured brush survived out here was a mystery, but in places there was more than enough of it to conceal at least one man and horse who might manage to get close to the Fielders' line of travel. By night, more than one man.

When they halted for a few minutes, Ord ladled out small drinks from the cask lashed to the back of his wagon, this to all but Alyard who shook his head and drank sparingly from his own canteen. Of the cask-water, Ord remarked, 'Jes' over half, still. Water-hole's say, three days. We kin top up when we git there.' Provided it wasn't dry.

In this wind Alyard had given up trying to see much. The entire flats seemed to be on the move. All stood with their backs to the wind until Ord motioned to them that it was time to get moving. Sarah looked at the black horse as though she would have preferred to travel on it with Alyard, but then turned and climbed back on to Ord's wagon. Henry threw his crutch back on to his own rig and deftly got himself back up on the seat. Alyard was watching him.

Suddenly, to Ord's back, and Hanni's, as they prepared to climb up on their wagon, Henry said, 'Clem . . . I didn't have no choice . . . ' Alyard was still staring at Henry. Close to babbling, blinking his eyes, brushing angrily at wind-blown grit, Henry said, 'It was real terrible, Ord, seein' Clem like that, hangin' there, burnin' an' screamin' an' tryin' to git hisself away from the fire . . . ' His voice cracking, he said, 'I didn't have no choice.'

Ord, looking back at Henry, said, ''S all right, Henry. Yuh done what had to be done.'

Hanni Fielder was looking at Alyard.

She might just as well have said outright, 'Why *wasn't it you that did it?*'

Alyard swung up, settled in the hot saddle. At the outset, Ord had said that if Alyard was heading the same way then they would be glad of his company. At that time, when Alyard had taken up the opportunity, Hanni had looked relieved. Grateful, even. But the rawness of danger could work on people in different ways. In Hanni's case it seemed to have turned into a kind of resentment directed more or less against Alyard, perhaps in part because of the way her brother had been acting. It was as though Henry was desperate to *justify* what had occurred back down the trail. Now, Alyard observed, Henry appeared to have fallen into one of his black moods, his narrow shoulders hunched over, his hat pulled down against the dust, looking only at his two-horse team.

Alyard, walking his horse, was ranging this way and that, cursing the wind-flung grit. After an hour or so, he came loping in close to Ord's wagon and waved him down to a stop. Alyard figured that to press on in these conditions was inadvisable. And the animals needed to be given water.

'We should stop, Ord. Wait for sundown. This wind'll prob'ly drop by then.'

'Yuh mean move at night?'

Alyard nodded. 'No cloud. Maybe not much of a moon. But enough.'

Henry had not got down off his wagon. He was lost in his own thoughts or plain uninterested in the reason for the halt or what Alyard and Ord might be talking about. Hanni and her daughters were staying under the canvas away from the uncomfortable conditions. Ord dragged a nickel-plated watch from a fob-pocket.

'Could be yuh're right at that. It was a mistake, pushin' on as far as this.'

So they made some kind of a camp under the wagons, which they brought side by side, close together. Henry turned very surly about it, hearing that it had been Alyard's opinion that they should wait until sundown before moving again. The females were hot, grittily uncomfortable and saying little.

After sundown they began stirring, shaking sand and grit from clothing, and relieved that, as Alyard had hoped, the wind had died away. Now there was an almost eerie quiet.

Sarah, clattering plates, ready to share out cold food, said, 'Look. 'Way over there.'

In what was a westerly direction there was a pinpoint of light, brightening, fading, brightening again.

'Camp-fire,' Henry muttered. It was a long distance away. 'Chapin.'

Once noticed, the wavering spark of light kept drawing their attention. They prepared to move on. In the gloom Ord pointed to a south-western constellation.

'We'll kinda keep that bright'n there ahead.'

Hanni and her daughters were about

to climb up on the wagon, then without uttering a word, Sarah broke from the group and, her skirts whispering, went across to where Alyard was already mounted. He could see the pale blur of her face as she held up a hand, and in the space of a moment or two she had settled in behind the bedroll. Alyard fully expected Hanni to voice some objection, but none came.

As they travelled along in the cool, almost windless night, none of them could resist looking from time to time at the distant, winking light. As time went by, however, the miles drifting under the wheels, it fell away behind on their right quarter, until it could scarcely be distinguished. Finally Sarah leaned forward, placing her hands on Alyard's back.

'I can't see it at all now, Tom.'

Alyard looked. She was right. It had gone. It was as though they had at last moved beyond Chapin's influence into a zone of safety. Even Henry called, 'Cain't see no light no more.' His tone, too, was saying that the immediate danger from the Chapin party was past. Henry seemed to have emerged from his dark mood. For the present.

Sarah said, 'Maybe they've really given up. You think that, Tom?'

Alyard saw no point in trying to put a better face on it, having had further thoughts about it.

'To me they didn't seem like the givin'-up kind. We need to keep a good watch all the time.' And he added, 'You better be the eyes in the back o' my head.' The girl laughed softly and just as gently punched him on the shoulder. It was the act of someone who felt totally at ease with another human being and Alyard warmed to it. Thereafter they conversed in low tones, Alyard moving the horse a few yards further away from the slow-moving, creaking wagons. He and Sarah were travelling in pleasant harmony, as though not only did Bob Chapin seem far away, but all others as well.

When light was streaking the eastern

sky, Ord reckoned that he had veered somewhat away from his intended south-westerly direction and pulled around accordingly. The wagons, the horseman and the girl up behind him could be distinguished plainly enough now. Alyard had fallen slightly behind.

When it came, the first rifle shot jolted them all out of somnolence. Hanni screamed. A second shot lashed out, the sound oddly dampened in this vast expanse of the flats. Ord was hauling hard on the long lines while Henry, coming to a stop, was pawing around behind him for the carbine. Alyard had swung Sarah down and he himself had dismounted, rifle in hand and, seemingly all in one motion, dragging the horse down and sideways, causing it to fall on its side. In the shortest of time, Alyard had forted up, one arm around Sarah's narrow shoulders, pressing her down behind the horse. He was desperately looking for something to shoot at.

Dimly, as another shot came, he

could hear Lilah screaming and Ord yelling something about water. Another shot. Alyard then let fly with the Winchester. He missed a running man some sixty yards away, a man emerging from behind brush and pacing alongside a horse, then steadying, trying to mount on the run. Alyard shot again and there was a furious flurry of dust, the horse screaming and going down, its legs thrashing. The would-be rider left it, running hard for cover. Alyard tracked him calmly and shot again and this time the running figure took the bullet, being punched by it and made into a wobbling marionette before going to ground, rolling, dust rising.

To Sarah, Alyard said, 'Keep well down.' To Henry, he shouted, 'Cover me!' Alyard went to the head of the black, hauling at the reins, slapping the animal hard as it rolled and came to its feet, shaking free of dust, its head wagging. Before Sarah could comprehend what was happening, Alyard was up in the saddle and driving the black horse forward, soon spurring it into a dead run towards where the man had gone down.

The shot horse was still thrashing and screaming, but Alyard rode hard beyond it to where its rider lay. He turned out to be the Mexican, Ramon Sanchez, and he was dead. Alyard picked up the man's rifle. Watchfully he retreated, returning to the thrashing horse which he dispatched with a single shot from his Winchester. Then he went directly to Ord Fielder and put Sanchez's rifle in the wagon. No one had been hurt. He told Ord who it was he had shot. Sarah now came to them, and Henry. Lilah was in a bad way and would not let go of Hanni.

The rest of them had now fallen very quiet. They might have come through unscathed but there was now a serious problem: the water cask had been struck twice. They had lost almost all of the water.

8

They waited at the wagons, trying to cover all directions at once. The sudden loss of the water was a devastating blow, but the possibility of another attack was an even more chilling threat. The wind was not as bad as it had been on the previous day but was still strong enough to raise plenty of dust and send it skimming across this table-flat expanse of country like a swiftly flowing tide. The heat was oppressive, and flies, large and green-backed, were pestering animals and humans alike.

The men out there somewhere were very dangerous. One of their number had been shot to death and it had to be assumed that the others would come seeking retribution. Though Ord raised another point.

'Mebbe they don't know about him, yet. Depends on how far away the rest of 'em are.'

Henry was of the opinion that Chapin and the others were not close by.

'By this time we woulda heeard some mouthin' off from Bob.' That did seem not unlikely. 'But if he is camped off some ways, when that goddamn' Mex don't show up, the whole passel of 'em's gonna come a-lookin'.'

Alyard offered no opinion. Ord came back to the serious question of the water.

'Two days, about, to the water-hole?'

'About that,' Henry reckoned. Hanni came. Again she raised the possibility of going back the way they had come. 'Long haul, either way, Han,' Henry said. He still had an odd look about him, as though haunted by the recollection of the blazing Clem Cotton and of his own part in what had occurred. Indeed, Henry was behaving strangely. Ord shook his head, looking at his wife.

'We come this far. I reckon we cain't do nothin' else but go on.'

Sarah and Lilah had been keeping watch from the opposite side of Ord's wagon. Now Sarah came to where she could see and hear what was being said.

Henry muttered, 'We keep on.' Then, 'Best we kin hope fer is to git to that water-hole not long afore sundown tomorrer.' Then he put into words what Alyard had had in his mind for a little while. 'If Bob gits it in his haid, he could be there ahead of us.'

Hanni started to say something. 'Surely he'd not — ' She stopped, knowing what she was about to say would sound absurd. If Chapin did get there ahead of the Fielders, and there was every chance that he would, there could be no doubt in anybody's mind that he would trade for water, nor what he would expect to get in exchange for it.

With a gloved hand, Alyard shoved back his hat. He took a long look around across the shifting dust and the shimmering distance. That no other movement could be seen meant nothing. Sanchez had got in close enough to destroy the water-cask. And with an ounce of better luck he would have got clean away with it.

'I'll go on ahead,' Alyard said. He slapped the neck of the black. 'This feller, he'll get me there. If they've already set out, but if they've not got too big a jump, I might get there ahead of 'em.'

Sarah seemed about to say something, then stopped and dropped her gaze, perhaps not wishing to cross words with her mother. Nonetheless, when she raised her eyes she kept them fixed on Alyard, and even when he climbed into the saddle and set the black loping away, stood watching until horse and rider had become only an image distorted by the dust and the heat-haze. When Henry muttered something she turned her head to stare at him. Henry had said, 'Could be the last we'll see of that bastard.'

Ord said, 'We got to hope it ain't. We need him an' we need that there rifle o' his'n.' It was true that Ord himself had acquired the one that had belonged to Sanchez, but Ord knew that he could not come anywhere close to Alyard's skill in using such a weapon.

'Cavalry,' mumbled Henry. 'The way he took that horse down an' forted up an' nailed that feller an' got it up ag'in an' move out real fast.'

After the wagons were moving again, an hour into the uncomfortable journey and travelling almost abreast, both Ord and Henry, exchanging hand-signals, were trying to decide whether or not, a long way across to their right, there was dust that was not merely wind blown. Eventually, nodding vigorously, Henry confirmed his opinion that there was indeed man-made dust out there, and remaining roughly at the same angle to their own progress. They were being shadowed.

Alyard had kept going as steadily as he could through the night, thankful for cooler conditions but pausing every hour or so to allow the horse to rest. From what remained of his canteen-water he moistened his lips, tipped the rest into his hat and gave it to the horse. It was quite inadequate but there was nothing Alyard could do about it. Everything depended on getting to the water-hole, then hoping that, first, they had not got there ahead of him, and second, that the water-hole had not dried up. If either were to be the case then Ord Fielder and his family would be in even deeper trouble.

With the new day, Alyard was within sight of the water-hole. Some greenish growth, brush and hardy grass, around its perimeter, offering hope of water to be had there. The black, indeed, had smelled it and was anxious to get there but, still wary, Alyard restrained the horse, even though there was no evidence of other riders.

It was just as well that he was cautious, for there came the flat snap of a rifle shot and dust jumped only a yard to the left of the horse. Alyard brought it to a stop and dismounted fast. Then, towing the animal, ran, angling away to gain more distance to get to the nearest, probably inadequate cover, behind a spiny, dried-up clump of brush. The rifle went off again and the bullet *whapped* crusted ground a few yards from him. Alyard reached the brush.

He did not stop there, however, but, tugging hard at the strung-out reins, ran on some forty yards and, as he had done when going after Sanchez, put the horse down on its side, dust rising. Alyard had gambled that the scrappy brush he had headed for would have screened his movements thereafter, and that the rifleman would assume that Alyard was closer than in fact he now was.

Such proved to be the case. During the following three minutes, four further shots were fired, all of them smashing through dry, thorny branches and falling well short of Alyard. Alyard took advantage of that and pulled and slapped the black to its feet and went jogging away, reins in hand, the duty horse going with him readily.

Alyard retreated another fifty yards, then sharply changed direction, heading to the right before angling in again. The sun was climbing higher in the sky but would be at his back and therefore shining in the face of whoever was at the water-hole. It was not much of an advantage but Alyard reckoned anything was better than nothing.

Alyard believed that he was up against only one man. Had there been the whole group he would have been mown down, him and the horse. Well, whichever this one was, he had been too hasty and possibly had been distracted by the shifting dust and the early sun-glare off these flats and by now he would sure be cursing his own folly. Allowing the horseman to come in for another dozen yards would have made all the difference. In Alyard's mind, this man, sent ahead, was therefore unlikely to be Bob Chapin himself. The Indian, Joseph Small Bear, would likely have shown more patience, greater cunning, leaving less to chance. That left Jack Drago. A hard, very dangerous man. Alyard knew that it would be unwise to rush him. Anyway, he did not know the man's exact position.

Alyard led the horse to some near-dead brush and tied it there. Winchester in hand he then moved off unhurriedly, crouching, eyes narrowed, peering through the shifting dust, working his way back towards the water-hole. Before long, Chapin and Joseph Small Bear would be bound to put in an appearance. Somehow he had to work out how he might drive Jack Drago from his position before they got there.

By now, however, Chapin might have observed that the horseman was no longer with the wagons and chosen to take on Henry Pedderson, with his carbine, while well aware that Ord Fielder was no hand with firearms, and whether or not Chapin knew that the rifle belonging to Ramon Sanchez had been taken by whoever had killed the Mexican. No doubt Chapin would be aware by now of the death of Sanchez and in all likelihood put that down to Alyard.

The day's rising heat was pressing down on Alyard as he lay looking towards the green brush surrounding the water-hole. It was some distance from him, sometimes completely obscured by dust, and between that place and Alyard were only a few clumps of poor vegetation. In this region only the hardiest of plant life could survive, and the brush, other than that around the water, was often skeletal. Hat pulled well down and his bandanna tied around nose and mouth, Alyard considered that the only chance he would have, to get in close to the other man, would be if the wind increased and more of the choking dust was raised. Yet Drago would be on the alert for any movement that could signal Alyard's approach, and even with the dust as occasional cover, Alyard knew that the next time that Drago got a sight of him he would be careful not to let fly too soon, make sure of getting a clean hit.

★ ★ ★

They came at the wagons from out of the filmy dust, two horsemen, Bob Chapin and Joseph Small Bear, not shooting at Ord's wagon, only at Henry's, causing him to fall behind, then stop, as he had to apply himself to using the carbine. Lead came slamming into the wagon. Henry fired, and fired again at the hard-riding horsemen.

Ord pulled his wagon to a stop, took the Sanchez rifle and got down, walking away from the vehicle. He shot at a dust-misted rider, but without much hope of hitting him. Ord's purpose in coming away from the wagon was an attempt to draw answering fire away from it and the females.

Henry was shouting to him. 'Git down, Ord! Fer Chrissake git down!'

Ord seemed not to hear him and continued walking slowly, shooting again. The carbine banged. Crouching along the neck of his horse, Joseph Small Bear fired a one-handed shot with a rifle and the bullet smacked into one of Henry's horses. Then, abruptly, the Indian changed direction, coming in head-on, now almost standing in the stirrups, shooting, and shooting again, then veering away. Now both of Henry's horses were down, thrashing dustily, Henry half falling from the wagon, scrabbling for his crutch with one hand, gripping the carbine with the other.

The riders vanished. Ord came closer to Henry's wagon, the two-horse team still thrashing about in a tangle of harness. Both animals were beyond help. Ord came to them and shot them. He backed away, then went back to assure himself that Hanni and his daughters had come to no harm.

Henry, still watchful, propped on the crutch, yelled to the dusty vastness, '*Bastards*!'

Ord, coming back, trailed by Hanni, Sarah and Lilah, said, 'Two, Henry. On'y two. Shoulda been three on 'em.' It caused Ord to make a slow circuit of the wagons, apprehensive that while Chapin and the Indian had been riding by, drawing all attention, Jack Drago might have been working his way in close, from another direction. But he could see no one.

When he came back to the group, Ord said, 'This is a goddamn' mess! We got to dump some of our stuff. Nothin' else fer it.'

So not only Henry's wagon with its contents and its dead team was abandoned to the dust-raked flats, but several items out of Ord's rig, this so that room could be made for Henry.

The sun was close to dipping below the horizon. Alyard had worked his way around to the western side of the water-hole, using the sun's last glare as, earlier, he had used it from the eastern side. But he was still some distance from the place. He had the rifle wrapped in his shirt to prevent any metallic glint giving away his position and was drawing himself along on his elbows. It was tough going, only small purchase for his boots, but he clenched his teeth and kept at it doggedly until the green brush was only some twenty yards ahead. At that point he stopped. Dust was matted all over his sweating body and caked around his eyes above the blue bandanna. Sunlight was still blazing behind him. He waited.

Then, there it was: a glint of metal. There, through the leafy branches. With the utmost care, taking his time, Alyard unwrapped the Winchester. Shooting through branches, the bullet might well be deflected. That, and the lack of a clear target meant that the chances of nailing the man were slim. But he must provoke some action, for if there had been no undue delay, the Fielder wagons must surely be seen soon.

The shot sounded flat, like two bits of wood being slapped together. Leaves and slivers of branches flew and there was some kind of flurry before an answering shot came. But it was a wild one, the bullet coming nowhere near Alyard, suggesting that the shooter had answered on reflex, with no real idea of where the other man was.

Alyard shot again, and this time thought he heard a cry. After that there was silence. Wary of a trap, he remained where he was, as flat as he could get, the sun behind him. A horse whickered. Then a rider came into view, bursting out of brush, the man quirting the horse strongly, heading across Alyard's line of vision, forty yards away, on the opposite side of the water-hole. In the quick impression he got, Alyard confirmed that it was Jack Drago and that there seemed to be something wrong with his near arm, the left one. Alyard propped, tracking the fast-moving horseman. He shot but missed. He let him go.

Winged the bastard, Alyard thought. In the last of the sun's rays he could follow the progress of the rider by the rising dust, since the wind had died somewhat and there was less wind-stirred dust around. He stood up. To the north-east he thought he could see something else on the move. On his way around the water-hole, heading towards the place where he had tied the black, he reckoned that what he could see was a wagon. But this was strange. Stare as he might, he could not see a second one.

9

In the moonless night they were at the water-hole, all the Fielders, Henry Pedderson and Tom Alyard, along with the remaining wagon. They had risked a fire, made coffee and a meal, but the flames had long since been doused, the water-hole and its environs returned to darkness.

Earlier, Ord Fielder, using plugs that he had shaped with a knife, had carried out makeshift repairs to the ruptured water-cask.

'Water'll swell them things,' he said, 'tighten 'em.'

The cask had been refilled. Hanni had also seen to it that some iron pots, with lids, had been filled with water and stowed inside the wagon. Alyard had filled his canteen. They had gone about it all without much talk, but Hanni, in the hiatus after the meal and the other activities, suddenly demanded of her husband an answer he couldn't give.

'Why, Ord? Why's Bob Chapin still comin' back at us an' back at us?'

Ord shrugged. 'It's got outa all reason, now, Han. Bob's pride ... I dunno. Anyways, he's a drunk. No ways can yuh talk sense with a drunk.' Wearily he shook his head. One drunk cowman, a wounded and vicious saddlebum and a still-savage Indian, no matter that he wore white-eyes clothing, yet they were out there, and not far away, waiting their chance to hit the wagoners again. It was the Indian who worried Ord the most.

The women looked to be close to exhaustion. Ord, Henry and Alyard himself were in little better case. In a sense, Henry was worse off. He was still blaming himself for the attack on the wagons, taking it back to the moment he had squeezed the shot away that had killed Clem Cotton. What he had said to Ord, earlier, came bursting out again now.

'But I didn't have no choice. Yuh see that, Ord? No choice.'

'I know it, Henry. Hanni too. We all do.' Ord slipped a glance at Alyard, who was standing with Sarah. It was as though the farmer was asking him to say something, but the dark-visaged man stared back at him implacably. They all set about preparing to rest, movements indistinct in the gloom.

The wagon was on the south side of the water-hole, just beyond some clumps of green brush, and with more brush on its western side. The wagon-team had been unhitched and watered and led back to be picketed a dozen yards from the wagon. Without a lot of discussion, and what there was in low voices, the people took up their places, Hanni sharing out some blankets. Henry, still muttering to himself, chose to stretch out not far from where the horses were. Hanni climbed inside the wagon. Before she did, she had a low-voiced conversation with Sarah. Perhaps she thought the girl might have followed Alyard, to sleep near where he slept. Sarah chose to sleep in the open on the western side of the wagon, a couple of yards away from it, while her younger sister crawled in beneath the vehicle. Alyard went nearer to the water-hole, having picketed the black with the wagon-horses, then made a circuit of the water and threw his bedroll down. In a brief exchange with Ord and Henry, Alyard had agreed to being awakened by Henry after four hours, until which time Henry would remain awake, watching, and listening for any sound which might mean that the Chapin party were on the move. It was a makeshift arrangement at best, but all that tired people could put together. But reason suggested that Chapin, Drago and Joseph Small Bear must also be in dire need of rest. Ord reckoned that they would have pulled back to what he called *out of range*, so they could do just that.

Henry's mind, left to himself, was still alive with disquieting images, not only of the hapless Clem Cotton, but others that had plagued him for much longer and were among the hideous entrails of the war. From time to time he had to shake himself to full awareness. His eyes sought to pierce the darkness, his ears attuned to every slight sound. There was a faint gleam coming off the flat water. No wind now stirred the leafy brush. The moon was obscured by cloud.

Henry wondered if, tomorrow, Chapin would come or, with Drago wounded — so Alyard had claimed — he might at last think better of it and pull out. Strange man, Bob Chapin. A drunk, maybe, like Ord had said, but a cunning one. Cunning enough to have lit and left burning a camp-fire, knowing that they must see it, distantly, and assume that Chapin had stopped to make a camp. But he must have still been on the move, tracking them. The horses were stirring. Henry, too, shifted, squinting into the dark, gripping the carbine.

The horses settled. Henry relaxed.

After, he did not know how long, Alyard, sliding into deeper sleep, came awake. On the far side of the water-hole the picketed horses seemed restive. He considered walking around there to reassure himself that the black was in no distress but the sounds soon ceased, and Alyard, too, relaxed. Every bone and muscle in his body was aching and his clothing was abrasive with grit. He was sure that he had hit Jack Drago, but how badly he could not know. Yet Drago had ridden out very hard, suggesting that he had not been badly hurt. So, three of them out there still. Alyard did not believe that they would let go now. A kind of compulsion had set in, Chapin worrying at them like a vicious terrier. So Chapin, Alyard was sure, would be back.

Little by little, weariness overcame Alyard. Four hours. That had been the arrangement, then Henry was to walk around and awaken him. A gentle quiet had fallen. There was a sense of the vastness of the land, of remoteness. Alyard's thoughts turned to Sarah Fielder. He had noticed where she had chosen to sleep through this mild night, after the first good meal in days. Now all that was needed was some hours of true rest, an escape, however brief, from the horrors of this journey. At one moment Alyard had thought that the girl would stay close to him, but perhaps Hanni had put an end to that notion. Alyard carried the image of Sarah's face into sleep.

How long he or any of them slept was not measured until afterwards, but what Alyard did know was that, even at his distance from the rest, he came out of sleep because of the scream. Blundering into wakefulness, Alyard realized that the high-pitched sound had not come directly from the campsite but from a little distance away.

When he came to his feet, the Winchester was in his hand. Over there near the wagon there was a great deal of confusion but in the darkness Alyard could see nothing. He could hear Henry's voice and Ord's, and he could hear Hanni, sounding alarmed and angry.

Alyard went jogging around the perimeter of the water-hole, and in the interests of self-preservation, called out, 'Henry? Ord?'

Even so, when he drew near to them the first intimation of Henry Pedderson's presence was the glint of the carbine's short barrel. But it was not Henry who spoke first, but Ord.

'She's gone! They got her!'

'What?'

'Sarah! They took Sarah!'

Hanni was shouting, too, and Lilah was crying. So it had been Sarah who had screamed. Just as Clem Cotton had been taken, Sarah had been taken. In the night. And in all probability by Joseph Small Bear. No one had heard anything. Nothing had been touched. The horses were restless now but only because of the urgent activity nearby. Hanni asked the question that had been pressing at Alyard's mind.

'Didn't yuh *hear* 'em, Henry? Didn't yuh hear *nothin*'?'

Now that the focus had shifted, even for a very short time, to Henry, it was enough to goad a man who was already very much on edge.

'I didn't *hear* nothin'! I didn't *see* nothin'!' He must have known that they thought he had fallen asleep. Probably he had.

Hanni was moving around here and there with little point, distraught, vaguely coming and going in the darkness. Ord had made as though to take hold of her but had been almost roughly thrust aside. Instead, Lilah, sobbing, found her father and he held her, crooning to her as he might have done to a much younger child. Since the one icy scream from Sarah there had been utter silence from the darkness beyond the water-hole. It was uncanny. There was the immediate sense of desperately wanting to do something while knowing that there was nothing that *could* be done. Chapin held the high card. Of course, he could simply ride away. Hanni said so now, but Alyard's opinion was that Chapin would not do that. Eventually they would hear from him. Chapin needed to replenish his canteens, for Alyard also believed that Drago had neglected to do so. And neither Drago nor the Indian would be satisfied to leave the other two females here.

But all Alyard said was, 'He needs fresh water for him an' the animals.' And did not add, *'An' that'll be the first thing he'll demand with his bargaining chip.'*

Ord thought that what Alyard had said was likely true. But if it was, then they were in for a long wait. And the more time that went by, without word, the more anxious did Hanni become. Ord did his best to settle her down, both her and Lilah, but it was clear that mother and daughter were near the end of their tether.

To Henry, Alyard said, 'I'll go take a

poke around. Take it easy with the carbine. I don't want my ass shot off, comin' back in.'

Standing in the gloom, face like a mask, Henry did not answer. Alyard vanished into the outer darkness. He moved slowly through the leafy brush, just a step at a time, but beginning a complete circuit of the water-hole. He saw nothing and indeed heard nothing until once again he drew near the Fielders' campsite. Henry near to shit himself when Alyard said, 'I'm back.'

Ord's voice enquired, 'That you, Tom?'

'Yeah.' He moved closer to the Fielders. 'Saw nobody, heard nothin' out there. Heard plenty from this place. I know this is a real bad situation, but we all need to stay quiet. Don't send out signals.'

Hanni, her voice much lower, asked, 'They *have* gone? They've took her?'

'I still doubt they've gone far,' Alyard said. Then, perhaps brutally, 'They need Sarah in good shape. To bargain with.'

'Bargain fer water,' Hanni said, 'an' bargain fer us.'

Ord with the Sanchez rifle, Alyard with his Winchester and Henry with his carbine, took up positions around but short distances away from the wagon, while Hanni and Lilah climbed inside it, to lie low. Alyard had said that, although he had scouted all around this place, failing to find anybody or hear anything, he was convinced that Chapin was not far off and was now playing on the nerves of the wagoners, in particular Hanni and Lilah. Blundering about in darkness would be highly dangerous, though every instinct leaned towards searching, trying to locate Sarah as quickly as possible. Yet they must wait for the sky to lighten. Reluctantly, the Fielders had accepted the sense of that over their desperate anxiety for their beloved girl.

Henry had said very little, whether because of a sense of culpability, Sarah vanishing while he had been supposedly on watch, or an even more brooding withdrawal into one of his dark moods, Alyard, of course, could not know. What he did know, through tone and gesture, — apparent even in the night — was that the one-footed man's antipathy towards him had by no means diminished.

They did not altogther maintain their positions. After an hour or so, Alyard sought out Ord and suggested that he get some rest.

'Me an' Henry, we'll sit it out. Come sun-up you can watch while we get some shuteye.'

Ord crawled in under the wagon. Then Alyard found Henry and told him. Henry seemed to accept it. At least he made no objection. Together they stood surveying the dark brush and the faint gleaming of the water. Some small animal, drinking there, went scuttling away. Other creatures would come, giving further evidence of life even out on these unappealing flats. Henry grunted, shifting his weight on the crutch. He must have seen the vague shape of Alyard's face turn towards him.

Low-voiced, Alyard asked, 'Where'd it happen?' His Southern accent seemed more pronounced.

'It don't matter where,' Henry said. 'It don't matter how. All done with. All dead an' buried.'

'Infantry?' Alyard enquired implacably.

For a moment or two he thought that he would get another curt answer but eventually Henry said, 'Yeah. Three-striper.' He stopped abruptly, then reverted to his customary manner when talking with Alyard. 'An' by God, I sent a few Johnny Rebs down the long road.' The tone was challenging. Alyard did not respond to it. Yet even in this enclosing darkness the agitation of the man was undeniable. Alyard moved away.

When the sky became streaked with light, Alyard's drooping head came up. It was several seconds before the tension drained out of him. His own failure to stay awake had left him vulnerable, exposed others to danger just as much as Henry's failure had done when Sarah had been taken. So Alyard's chagrin was deep and immediate.

The water-hole and the green brush and the wagon could now be picked out clearly. And there was some slow activity at the wagon. Alyard could see Ord there, then Hanni and Lilah. Ord was getting ready to light the fire. Alyard looked around but could not see Henry. Nor, beyond the brush, were there any more distant signs of anybody else. The wind had not yet come up, so there was no dust. Alyard went pacing towards the wagon. Hanni's face was drained of colour. Stricken. It seemed she hated herself for having slept while still not knowing where Sarah was and what had happened to her. Ord, seemingly, had done his best to comfort his wife but without success, not surprisingly, since his mind would be as turbulent as hers. There was an atmosphere of frustration, helplessness.

Seeing Alyard, Ord asked, 'Where's Henry?'

Alyard shrugged. 'He'll not be far.' He hoped that was the case. Unasked questions were in the eyes of the Fielders. Alyard let them remain unasked and went to check on the black and on the wagon-horses. When he came back, Henry was walking towards the group at the wagon, where blue brushsmoke was now threading into the air.

Henry said. 'Somebody comin'.'

Sure enough, out beyond the water-hole, maybe still 500 yards away, dust was puffing around the feet of a bunch of slowly incoming horses. Alyard, squinting, trying to count them, blinked and tried again. Presently, he said, 'If it's Chapin, an' I reckon it is, he's picked up more company. There's more'n four.'

10

The incoming party came to a halt some 150 feet from where Alyard, Ord Fielder and Henry Pedderson, all armed, had now gathered. Henry had called out, "Bout far 'nough, Bob!'

But it was not certain that this was the reason that the Chapin party had stopped. Now it could be seen who was who. Two men were mounted, two afoot, leading their horses. And on the end of a lariat that was attached at one end to a saddle horn, and tied by her wrists, was Sarah Fielder. Her clothing and her hair dishevelled, she was standing now with her head hanging.

Hanni screamed, 'Sarah!' She would have gone running forward had not Ord turned and urgently waved her back.

The fourth man in the party, one sitting a buckskin, was not unknown to at least one at the water-hole.

'That's one on 'em! One on 'em that woulda took me, at the farm!' Lilah would never forget any of them.

Henry grunted. He, too, it seemed, had instantly identified this unkempt newcomer. Alyard, his eyes half closed, had also fastened his attention on this man who now allowed the buck-skin to go slow side-stepping until it was standing almost side on to those gathered at the water-hole.

'Wa-al now! Cap'n Alyard, no less!' The accent was undeniably deep South. 'Sure 'nough is a small world!' He had bean-like eyes and round-the-mouth whiskers and a deeply lined, grimy face.

Narrow-eyed, Alyard nodded. 'Reeder.' Henry shot a glance at Alyard who was continuing to stare at the man on the buckskin. Alyard said, 'Long ways from home, Reeder, an' couldn't be in worse company.'

'Where I am an' who I'm with ain't none o' your business no more, Cap'n. An' if it's comp'ny yore all concerned about, wa-al, I reckon that'n there, with the carbine, he'd be an ol' blue-ass boy. Yep, if ever I did see one. What there is left of 'im. Now, Cap'n, I sure never did reckon to find yuh bumpin' knees with one o' them bastards. Specially knowin' what I know.'

Levelly, Alyard said, 'Long time ago, the war, Reeder.'

Reeder laughed.

Now Ord Fielder raised his voice, 'Sarah! They laid a hand on yuh, girl?'

Still looking down, long dark hair spilling on either side of her face, her own hands bound, the girl shook her head.

Chapin said, 'But she's standin' where she is, Ord, an' yuh're standin' where you are. Cain't git away from that nohow. But there's no use to have shootin' here. We'd both of us come out losin' if it come to that.'

'You sure would, anyways, Bob,' Henry said, twitching the carbine which was more or less lined up on Chapin.

'Henry, yuh're sure 'nough wed to that thing,' Chapin observed. Then,

'Ord, it's water I come fer.'

'Turn my girl loose,' Ord said. The farmer was sweating and Alyard considered he could be real close to doing something stupid. Hanni Fielder was gripping one of the hands of her younger daughter.

Surprisingly, Chapin said then, 'Could well come to that, Ord. But there's a tag to it.'

'Spit it out,' said Henry. His voice was low, husky with anger.

'Pleasure,' said Chapin. 'First thing is, that hang-dog bastard there, he'd best mount up an' git gone.' It was blunt confirmation that he was very apprehensive of Alyard.

Reeder was still shaking his head. 'Cain't nohow work it out, Cap'n, findin' yuh here sidin' some blue-ass an' a no-'ccount sodbuster.'

In a quiet voice, the words directed at Ord, Alyard said, 'If it'll make the difference, I'll pull out.'

'Bob, he ain't no ways to be trusted,' Ord said.

'Right now it's all you've got,' said Alyard. The sight of Sarah, the state of her, was tearing at him. He let his eyes shift from man to man in the Chapin group: Chapin himself, sneering, feeling confident now; Joseph Small Bear, impassive as always; Jack Drago, afoot, standing at the head of his horse, his upper left arm heavily wrapped with a dirty bandanna. And Reeder, sitting his buckskin, waiting for whatever windfalls there might be. A real bad soldier, an inveterate troublemaker, oily, vicious and without conscience. Deep unease stirred in Alyard. He could have well done without Caleb Reeder.

Henry now spoke to Ord. 'Let Alyard go, like he says, Ord. We don't need Alyard.'

Yet Ord could be a stubborn man. 'Even if Tom goes, there's no guarantee Bob Chapin's gonna give up Sarah.' They all knew that, having got hold of the girl, who all along had been

Chapin's irresistible lure, it seemed highly unlikely that he would release her.

Yet Alyard said to Ord, 'Best you do as he wants. That's my opinion.'

'What he wants is to take one rifle out,' Ord said.

'Maybe,' said Alyard. 'But if it does come down to a shoot, nail Chapin, right off. An' be sure you nail that Indian. Drago's been hit. Caleb Reeder's a low-life but his mouth's the best thing he's got. Go ahead, Ord. Tell Chapin.'

Ord licked his lips. 'Bob?'

'I hear yuh.'

'He'll do it. Alyard. He'll pull out. It ain't his fight.'

Alyard turned and walked unhurriedly to where the black was picketed, and once there, scabbarded the rifle. Even passing close by, he had not glanced at Hanni and Lilah.

To the surprise of the Fielders, Chapin and his companions, taking with them the roped girl, now began retreating. They went back a matter of fifty yards before stopping again. Maybe Chapin wished to get a longer view, beyond the waterhole, so that he could see exactly what Alyard did once he had moved away.

What Alyard did was ride south-westward. There would be times at which, because of some clump of brush, he would not be clearly in view and, as the distance lengthened and the dust blew — as it was starting to do now on a small, lifting breeze — his shifting image would become less distinct. He rode steadily on. Not until he had covered several miles did Alyard bring the black to a halt and get down. All around him stretched the now filmy expanses of Deadman's Flats, dotted with the sorry-looking brush. But in the more distant south-west, against a pale sky, was faintly etched the line of the Sligh Hills. Alyard led the nodding black to some near-dead brush and tied it, patting its long neck. He then walked some hundred feet away and, hunkering down, settled in to wait. He wondered who Chapin would send.

Time passed. It became more difficult to see for any great distance. The drifting dust offered an odd illusion, scattered brush briefly given false animation. Yet eventually the man did come, walking his horse through the yellowish veil. What he saw first was the picketed black. That caused him to draw his own mount to a stop. Cautious. Still fifty yards out, he must have been able to glimpse the black only intermittently. He was not all that bright, yet just fly enough to wonder why the black would be there, with no sign of its rider. The man suddenly turned and headed away again.

Alyard, grasping the Winchester, figuring he had not had a clear enough target, swore softly, for now there was nothing to see except the dust-curtain. He began shifting sideways, focusing on the place he had last seen the horseman. And it had not been the man he had expected. Still uncertain, he was straightening, preparing to make his way across to the black when the rider came looming out of the murk and giving vent to a high-pitched yell and shooting one-handed, with a rifle. Alyard shot but missed even as a fire-rod raked his left side, and he dropped to one knee.

Again the rider came and went, rifle lashing, Alyard shooting too, levering, shooting again, but all of it too hurried, not shooting well. With a sense of anger and frustration he knew that he might well come off second best here. His bloodied shirt sticking to his side, he still contrived to keep moving but did not know where next the rider might suddenly appear. Then he heard him again. Almost on top of him.

★ ★ ★

Henry was cursing the dust and cursing Bob Chapin. Expecting him to move in right after he was satisfied that Alyard had gone, there had been no sign of his coming. Ord had taken it as evidence of some sort of duplicity.

'Why else would he hang back, Henry? Alyard's gone. He knows it. He don't want to give up Sarah. That's it. He didn't never figure to.'

Hanni said, 'Oh God, Ord, what are we gonna do?'

'Wait,' Ord said. ''S all we kin do. He wants water as bad as all that, he's gotta make a move some time. But he'll come in fast, I reckon, use this damn' dust, git in real close afore we know it.' What he did not say was that Chapin might use Sarah to get him right in, put her at risk if Henry started cutting loose with the carbine. Yet Chapin wanted Sarah very badly. Somehow it did not seem reasonable, when you thought about it, that he would risk her in that way. Maybe that was why he had not tried to use her, right off. Time went on and still Chapin did not come.

But he was there, right enough, he and his party hunkered down, bandannas pulled up as defence against the choking dust. Sarah was unbound, now, with a stinking Indian blanket over her head. Jack Drago, in some pain with his arm, had wanted to get the business over and done with but Chapin refused to be pushed to it.

'Gotta be real sure, Jack. Sure that Alyard bastard ain't gonna show up ag'in. An' sure we nail Henry afore he nails one of us. It'll come though, all in good time.'

Drago had reverted to his hunched-up, brooding resentment and had drunk the last of the water from his own canteen. Still the wind was lifting the goddamn' dust and the water-hole and its rim of greenish brush was totally obscured.

Chapin was aware that Drago had begun to see the reluctance to move in on Ord and Henry as a sign of weakness. After all, the girl had been taken. She represented the highest card there was. Drago would never be able to understand why Chapin had held back from playing it. Chapin, squinting at the girl's huddled shape, could never have explained it to the likes of Jack Drago. Chapin wanted her, sure; but he also wanted her to *like* him. When he had appeared at that farm with his hair slicked down and his hopes — lit by a certain amount of alcohol — high, he had been humiliated. He would never forget the rest of them, for that. Yet it had not altered his feelings for *her*. So he had raged against Ord. He had fulminated over Henry Pedderson, but his longing for this pretty farm girl had never wavered. He was unable to understand why she could not respond to him. At the merest touch she had pulled away as though scalded. His low-voiced words had been received with contempt.

'I'll look after yuh, girl. I'll watch out fer yuh. None better. Jes' yuh tell yore pa, an' we kin all go our ways, peaceable.' But she must have known that at best it was no more than a half truth. The others were awaiting their share. Her mother and her sister. No other reason on earth for them still to be here.

Chapin came to his feet. Somewhere out in the gliding wall of dust a man had called, 'Bob!'

Drago stirred himself.

Chapin said, 'Spread out.' He grasped Sarah by an arm. As a matter of course she resisted but inevitably went with him. The girl had been waiting for any chance that might come to make a run for it. Now it seemed it was too late. Now the other man was back, of that she felt sure. And that must mean that Alyard was dead.

11

Chapin, Joseph Small Bear and Jack Drago had spread out somewhat, preparing to deal with anything unexpected. Chapin had told Sarah to crouch down, this some ten yards from where he was. Chapin himself was trying to settle the picketed horses. It was several minutes before he managed to get it done. The dust was drifting, thinning and thickening by turns. Again the call came.

'Bob?' He was quite certain that it had not come from anyone at the water-hole. For one thing the direction was wrong. Chapin, turning from the horses, had a bandanna pulled up and also had a hand raised to defend against the blown grit.

Suddenly, there was a horseman. Though he was indistinct, Chapin had the quick impression of a reddish shirt, but it was the horse that he recognized instantly. A buckskin.

'By God, Reeder, yuh got it done! Yuh nailed the bastard!' And to those unseen, he yelled, 'He *done* it, boys! He's took that bastard Alyard!' The buckskin-mounted man came closer and, when he got level with Sarah Fielder, she crouching, shaking with hopeless tears now, having listened to what Chapin had said, he swung down. Chapin, still delighted, even performed a kind of bobbing dance. He was laughing. 'We got all the bastards dead to rights now!'

The next moment, however, shaking his head, his laughter dying, dashing gloved hands at his eyes, he was struggling to comprehend what was happening. The red-shirted rider had got hold of the girl and was boosting her up on to the buckskin. He managed it but the horse grew fractious, retreating, throwing its head up, defeating the efforts of the man to remount. The man's hat had blown away. It was then that the truth hit Chapin but he was in two minds, unable to decide whether to go forward or back. Not managing to get back up on the horse, the red-shirted man gave the animal's rump a sharp smack and yelled to Sarah, 'Go!'

By this time Chapin was trying to get his pistol cleared away, but in his haste, was fumbling. Then the dust intervened and there was no longer a clear target anyway. Chapin screamed, 'It ain't Reeder! It's Alyard!'

The dust thinned. Now there was no sign of horse, girl or Alyard. Or was there? Yes! There! The man, afoot, pistol in hand. Chapin shot at him but was much too quick, too anxious. The target melted away, unscathed. Drago, somewhere over to Chapin's left was calling out, 'Where's he at?'

'Over here!' Chapin yelled, counting on Drago's sense of direction by sound. Joseph Small Bear did not call but Chapin had not expected him to. That did not prevent the Indian from putting in an appearance ahead of Drago and only a few yards away from Chapin. Chapin said, 'He was out yonderways. Got to git 'twixt him an' the water-hole!' The Indian slipped away, vanished in dust. Drago, his big face haggard, his left arm obviously paining him, was all for closing in fast. Now.

★　★　★

Ord Fielder had had enough. He had seized the rifle that had been taken from Sanchez and was set on going out to find his daughter. Hanni, distraught, wanted him to do it yet was terrified of his going.

'What hope yuh got of findin' her, in this?' They were huddled beneath the wagon, Henry too. Alyard was long gone, yet Chapin had not moved in. Or at least they had not seen him or any of his party. The woman's hands were pressed to her face. 'What's happenin' to her, Ord? What's happenin' to our girl?'

Henry made a comment that was unexpected. The collar of his shirt pulled up, the carbine held upright before him, he said, 'It's Bob that wants Sarah. He'll take her away. Back across the flats, mebbe. Them other fellers, they'll not git near her.' There was a strange comfort in this thought and even Hanni now fell quiet.

Presently Ord said, 'They cain't leave it a lot longer afore they come in fer water. They'll fetch her along, like afore, make sure we don't shoot.'

Henry said, 'They was real leery of that Alyard. Cap'n. That's what that feller called 'im. I knowed it. Johnny Reb. Cavalry.'

'Alyard sure did keep his eyes pinned on you, Henry,' Ord remarked. That was true. The mongoose and the snake.

Suddenly Lilah said, 'Look!'

Some way off, a rider had come out of the murk, then all but vanished again. Ord said sharply, 'By God! I'd swear it was Sarah!'

They all shouted her name. Maybe she had lost direction and would go riding out across the wilderness of the flats. She did not reappear.

Henry went scrambling out awkwardly from under the wagon, dragging his crutch. Ord, Hanni and Lilah came out, Lilah ignoring Hanni's instruction to stay where she was. Again, all together, they shouted Sarah's name. Nothing. Horse and rider had gone. Somewhere out in the drifting dust there was a gunshot. Henry said it was from a pistol.

Then quite close at hand, there was the rider on the buckskin horse.

'Sarah!'

Ord swept her down, the girl almost falling into his arms. Hanni clutched at her.

'Oh my God! My Sarah!'

She was filthy and trembling and half blinded by the gritty dust. Henry made an attempt to grab the buckskin but it evaded him and headed for the water.

Several minutes passed before they could get much out of Sarah, Hanni sponging her face with a wet cloth, gently wiping her eyes.

'Mr Alyard . . . Tom. He's come back . . . '

'What?' Ord could not take it in.

With some difficulty, Sarah said, 'They sent . . . that man after him . . . that Reeder. That's his horse. Tom come back on it, wearin' some of Reeder's clothes. He fooled Bob Chapin just long enough to get me away.'

There came the sound of more gunshots. They thought they could hear voices shouting but the words were indistinguishable. Henry, propped on his crutch, grasping the carbine, told them harshly to take cover.

'If yuh kin git it done, Ord, afore they come at us, hitch the team. Git ready to pull out. Catch that there buckskin an' tie 'im on behind. We stay here much longer, we'll be here 'til our bones turn white.' It was now clear that he was preparing to go out looking for Alyard.

'Henry, it's too goddamn' risky,' Ord said.

Henry shook his head. 'They nail him quick, they'll come straight fer us. It cain't last.'

Ord knew it to be the truth and had to be faced. He watched sadly as Henry, buffeted by the wind and whipped by the stinging dust went swinging away.

★ ★ ★

Because Alyard was unable to see the thicker brush that rimmed the water-hole, the dust having thickened, he had for the moment lost his sense of direction. At any time he might go blundering into one of them, or worse, be seen briefly and stalked by them, unseen. There had been a sharp exchange of fire, targets that had been, for each of those involved, mere shadows, evaporating almost as soon as they had manifested themselves.

For Alyard, this situation was uncannily akin to another, a skirmish long in the past, some of his troop down, along with their horses, having been lured into a wind-raked, dry riverbed, a scouting foray that had gone wrong, bitten off more than they could chew. He had lost five men, two of them good NCOs. Alyard, no matter that it had not counted against him later, had nonetheless carried some guilt with him ever after. *Error of judgement*. But that was among a number of things that had happened during the war that continued plaguing Alyard and others like him. It was one of them, through no more than a chance remark, that had fetched him into this territory in the first place. And that matter remained unresolved.

He dropped to one knee. He was straining to penetrate the drifting curtain, almost certain that he had caught a movement across to his right.

Indeed, there it was again.

Alyard had lined up the pistol and was on the very brink of letting go a shot, but something made him hold off. Something about the attitude of the figure he had glimpsed. Alyard moved cautiously in that direction.

'Henry?'

The man with the crutch came swinging out of the murk.

'Come near to nailin' yuh, Alyard.' He was holding the carbine in his right hand as he would a pistol. He said, 'The girl come back.' Alyard was relieved. Henry asked, 'Who's out here now, 'sides Bob?'

'Jack Drago an' the Indian. The other one, Reeder, he was the one they sent.' Alyard shrugged. 'The buckskin was his.' He did not bother recounting the last split-second of pistol fire that had seen Caleb Reeder hit in the left eye.

'Where's yore black?'

Alyard waved a hand vaguely. 'Out there. Had to leave 'im. Didn't want to be held back.'

179

Henry said, 'Ord's gittin' ready to pull out. They ain't come near. We got the wagon an' that buckskin an' plenty o' water. We got to take our chances.'

They were not nearly back to the water-hole before Jack Drago came lurching out of the dust, shooting. Alyard shot back. Drago fired again, then faded. Ahead of Alyard, Henry Pedderson kept swinging on, occupied with keeping his balance in the buffeting wind. It was not until they had covered another dozen yards that Alyard realized that Henry had been hit. There was a line of blood, dust-powdered now, across the back of his shirt.

'Not close enough,' Henry said. 'Ol' Jack, he warn't good enough.' Alyard cast a glance over his shoulder and let fly at a shadow. 'Git 'im?' Henry asked.

'No.'

'There's the wagon,' Henry said. Ord had done well to get the four hitched up. Hanni was in the act of leading the buckskin, loose-cinched but with

Alyard's saddle and scabbarded rifle still on it, towards the back of the wagon. When she saw Alyard and Henry coming through the murk, she stopped.

Ord called, 'Once we're on the move, they'll likely come at us.'

'They'll come at us on the move or not,' Henry said. He recognized as surely they all must have, that long since, the invisible line that made once-ordinary men into outlaws, had been crossed by Bob Chapin and that there could be no chance whatsoever of his crossing back. Maybe the poison had already been there, in the blood. Envy, greed, hatred and humiliation had nudged it into life through his rejection by a captivating farm girl.

Sarah had gone at once to Alyard and in a quick gesture touched him as though for reassurance that he was all right. Hanni was urging Henry to get up on the wagon and strip off his shirt, and even before he had done so, was fetching a wet cloth to clean the shallow stripe raked across his back. Lilah was already up inside the rig. Alyard urged Sarah to go join her sister and to lie as flat as they could. He tightened the cinches and remounted the buckskin and soon went loping away from the now-moving wagon.

The bullet-score in Alyard's side, put there by the mouthy but inadequate Reeder, had tightened up and was tending to slow his movements. It was a disadvantage he could ill afford. Weary and half choking in the dust, Alyard knew that whatever start the wagon family might get while Chapin and his companions slaked thirsts and watered horses, would soon enough count for little once a refreshed party set out after them. He had considered laying down some rifle fire to hold Chapin back from the water-hole but had discarded the notion. In the long run it could make little difference and would carry a high risk of his getting hit again. And with three of them coming in at him, too great a chance of his being outflanked and caught in crossfire.

Departing, looking back, and before a thick curtain of dust intervened, Alyard saw the first of them arriving at the water-hole.

12

The Fielder wagon was a couple of miles on before the first attack came. There was no warning because the blowing dust had concealed the approach of the riders. Alyard had done his utmost to get some early sight of them but realized, hollowly, that their comparatively easy mobility and speed would count very much in their favour when the time came.

And the conditions were in their favour. When they did come, they were no more than vague shadows, appearing and disappearing, shooting and pulling away again. But there was a rough strategy to it. They were keeping off to one side of the wagon, all of them, none coming around the opposite side. Clearly they were taking care not to put themselves in danger from their own crossfire. And they were perhaps still somewhat wary of the carbine in Henry Pedderson's hands.

Henry, in fact, had rolled back part of the hooped canvas covering to give himself a better view all around. He was kneeling on his good leg and already he had let fly at the hard-riding raiders. No doubt they were wary, too, of Alyard and in particular of his ability to range around freely.

When the first sweep of the horse-men came, Ord might have hesitated, even come to a halt, but Henry was constantly urging him to keep rolling. Henry knew that it was not going to make a spit in hell's difference whether they stopped or not. Stopping might offer a sense of forting up, but once they had done it they might never move on again.

Henry also yelled to the women to get down as far as they were able and to keep as much stuff as possible between themselves and the sides of the wagon. This was a different Henry. It was as though he had flung off like a cloak the dark mood that was so often upon him and was now prepared for pitched battle. Perhaps what they were seeing and hearing was the Henry of long ago, the one who, little more than a boy, had gone smiling off to war, eager to get within sound of the guns. The unsuspecting Henry.

Alyard, pistol in hand, was weaving the buckskin back and forth, trailing the wagon, unwilling to go riding off in pursuit of any of them, lest in the subsequent confusion and blasting exchanges, Henry mistake him for one of the Chapin party. But Alyard was keeping an occasional eye behind them as well, and soon enough saw at least one horseman looming there and shot at him, though without result other than to drive him back and out of sight again. There had been a fleeting impression of long hair and a coloured headband. Joseph Small Bear.

Hardly had that fierce apparition come and gone than Alyard's attention was grabbed by the further discharge of

Henry's carbine. That man was still steadying himself as best he could, down on one knee in the moving wagon. He was doing his utmost to track targets he could barely see and then only for mere fractions of a second. Appearing and vanishing, like other horsemen in the past, along misty creek-bottoms. Most times Henry did not shoot, knowing he would be wasting precious ammunition. Just the occasional one to give them a hurry-up.

Lead came whanging into the wagon and went whining off an iron wheel-rim. Crouching as he drove, Ord, too, was now calling for Hanni and the girls to keep their heads down, probably an unnecessary exhortation. Powerless, seeing nothing, hearing the intermittent shooting and a hit or two on the vehicle must have been unnerving. The creaking wagon went rolling on, amid the dust.

Chapin came, swinging in, surprisingly close, looking as though he was about to attempt to get alongside the leaders. Coming in, he shot at Henry, the most obvious target, but came close to hitting the driver, then went veering away as abruptly as he had arrived. Henry reckoned to himself that they must have had some liquor left and that Chapin had been at it, for it had seemed a most foolhardy move. If Henry had been better able to steady himself he might well have nailed the man. But it was no easy matter to keep enough balance on the lurching wagon and handle the carbine effectively.

Alyard now came spurring up alongside but he was much too late to get a shot at Chapin. Henry merely shook his head in frustration and Alyard went wheeling away again to drop back and trail the rig.

It was an unhappy coincidence that as Alyard fell back by about twenty yards, a horseman came hammering into view and suddenly was between Alyard and the wagon, with Henry somewhat unsighted and relying on Alyard to cover them in that direction.

Now Alyard could not risk shooting lest he himself hit the wagon. The rider who had so quickly appeared was Jack Drago, controlling the horse awkwardly with his left hand and holding a long pistol in his right. Drago fired at the wagon, then at Alyard. Alyard was not hit but the buck-skin was, and unluckily. Its head was whacked by the heavy lead and the animal at once knuckled over and spilled its rider, Alyard falling heavily, rolling over and over, losing the Colt Frontier as he did so.

Drago had gone riding on beyond the place from which he had shot at Alyard, but in the mist of yellow dust, as he was dazedly trying to drag himself upright, Alyard could see that the horseman, albeit clumsily, for he could not use one of his arms properly, was coming around for another approach. Covered in dust, every bone in his body shaken by the fall he had taken, Alyard was looking around desperately for the Colt but failing to find it. There was one other chance. He went crawling towards the still-quivering horse but it had come down on its right side and the scabbarded rifle was trapped under it. Drago was on his way back.

Alyard had to make one more try, take a last chance. He went diving to the ground, away from the horse, sweeping one arm back and forth ahead of him. He thought it was all to be for nothing and that at any instant a gunshot must send him to Eternity. Then his questing hand encountered the dust-covered pistol.

Drago must have seen that Alyard, coming now to his knees, had a pistol in hand, for he pulled the horse to one side to go veering away. Drago was definitely having some trouble handling the horse, his left arm not a lot of use. Alyard shot at Drago and though the horseman very soon passed from sight, thought that he might have hit him.

Shaken, dizzy, his wounded side afire now, Alyard was in some difficulty. And whether or not Drago had been hit, the man knew that Alyard was now afoot and away from the Fielder wagon and perhaps even realized that he had been unable to get at his rifle. Alyard went again to the fallen and now quite still buckskin for the purpose of trying to retrieve the Winchester. If he had had his full strength he would probably have managed it, but in his present state he had little hope. The full weight of the dead horse was on top of it and though he did his best to burrow an arm in and get hold of the weapon, he could not make it. Sweating and weakened as he was, he gave up. His senses were swimming but he dare not simply lower his head and rest. He might never be able to get up again.

Gathering himself, gripping the Colt, he got unsteadily to his feet. Swaying a moment or two, breathing deeply but almost choking in dust, he went staggering away, expecting to encounter at any second another of the marauding riders.

How far ahead of him the Fielders' wagon might be Alyard could only guess and he went blundering blindly through the murk in its tracks. Somewhere up ahead there sounded several gunshots and he recognized the sound of Henry's carbine among them. Alyard now did his best to work up to a jogging pace but was making heavy weather of it. He was conscious that Jack Drago might have got clean away and be close by. Then Alyard did catch a glimpse of a mounted man but it was not Drago. It looked more like the Indian. Blundering along, his side paining him badly and still very shaken from the fall from the horse, Alyard had begun to believe that he had made a bad misjudgement and had gone off in the wrong direction. He ought to have found them by now.

Suddenly, though, the wagon was revealed. It had come to a stop. Henry was now down off the vehicle and so were the Fielders. It would emerge that they had been first slowed down and then brought to a halt because of a series of persistent attacks by Bob

Chapin and the Indian, those two riding in at the leaders, bumping them and unsettling them. Chapin's purpose, his risk-taking, was to bring about this very halt, the object being to make one last strong bid to separate the men and the women. Chapin would have no way of knowing just how much ammunition Henry, in particular, might have, but would be prepared to gamble that it could not last much longer. Alyard was still an unknown quantity and clearly it had been Jack Drago's task to cut him out of the group, prevent him from rejoining the fight. There was now no sign of him.

When Alyard was still some forty yards away, a brief thinning of the dust revealed him to Henry Pedderson. Indeed it was Henry who, the carbine propped on the crutch, suddenly called something Alyard couldn't hear and made an arm motion, meant as an urgent warning.

Too late, Alyard turned, only to realize that Drago's horse was all but upon him. Even as he swayed back and tried to hurl himself from its path, one of the animal's shoulders struck him hard and he was flung backwards. Very close to him, Drago's pistol blasted and as he went tumbling away Alyard know only too well that he had been hit. His left arm was numbed. His own pistol was still gripped in his right hand.

The horseman had gone riding on, perhaps believing that he had well and truly nailed the man afoot. There was now no sign of him. Dazedly Alyard was doing his utmost to regain his feet but not making much headway. His left arm had warmed with blood. The shirt-sleeve was sodden with it. Alyard tried to focus on the wagon and Henry Pedderson, who had done his best to give him a warning, but could not. Nonetheless, having managed to get himself to a standing position he now took a pace in the direction he knew the wagon to be. His vision was clearing, but slowly. He looked up. Drago was coming back at him.

Alyard was struggling to raise the Colt. Waveringly he pointed it at the oncoming horseman but the hammer fell on a spent shell. Drago came on. Alyard saw that Drago, although wounded and still having problems controlling the horse, would have no trouble riding right over the top of him.

Then through the dust, swinging along with the aid of the crutch, came Henry Pedderson, bellowing at Jack Drago, who by now must have seen him off to one side. Indeed Drago, heading in towards Alyard, intent upon the kill, for here was the man who had wounded him at the water-hole, took a fly shot at Henry, mainly to deter him. Henry had got the carbine propped on the crutch and now he let fly.

The lump of lead whacked into the crouching rider and knocked him sideways in the saddle. But the impact did not unseat him. Swaying, he rode on. Henry levered, reloading, no doubt wanting to get in another shot before Drago vanished from his sight.

At that instant Joseph Small Bear came rushing at him, suddenly, yipping and whooping, shooting at him with a long, old-fashioned pistol. Henry was hit. Yet, snarling, he was doing his best to get the carbine lined up. The Indian, however, his coarse black hair flying, went by too quickly, so Henry failed in his attempt to get a clean shot. He did not fire at all.

Alyard, having been struck heavily by the horse, and his bloodied left arm hanging limply, set out to crawl towards Henry Pedderson who was now, as far as Alyard could make out, trying desperately to keep himself upright by means of the crutch. Alyard, in pain and almost blinded by sweat and dust, set his teeth and compelled himself to continue moving. It was agonizingly slow going.

He was still a few feet short of Henry when Sarah came. She hurried to Alyard first but he shook his head.

'No. See to Henry . . . '

For the one-footed man was in very

bad shape. How he had managed to stay even partly upright for as long as he had was nothing short of astonishing. All over his chest dark blood was glistening. A worm of it was finding its way down from the corner of his mouth. Henry's eyes were clouded, vacant now, but he found the strength to say, 'Bastard . . . Injun!'

Alyard realized that he had lost the Frontier Colt. Henry's carbine had at last left the hands of its owner and lay nearby. To Sarah, Alyard said, 'Pick that thing up an' don't let it out of your hands. Any one of 'em comes in sight, just let fly.' Whether or not she would, Alyard had no idea, for as far as he knew she had no experience of firearms. Maybe it would not make any difference anyway. The whole thing was slipping away from them now. Drago might well have been hit hard by Henry, but Bob Chapin and Joseph Small Bear were still out there somewhere, circling, calling the tune.

And here was one of them now

looming out of the gliding murk.

Alyard yelled, 'Sarah!'

The girl stopped and swung the carbine. The weapon blasted and Sarah all but lost control of it. The discharge of the weapon had been involuntary and she had hit nothing, but the unexpected firing was sufficient to send the incoming rider, Joseph Small Bear, pounding on and away, out of sight, the Indian crouching over the neck of the horse as he went.

It could not last. Now there was only Ord and the women. The wagon party was systematically being cut to pieces. When Sarah came back Ord wanted her to stay with her mother but the girl ignored him and left the carbine alongside a wheel of the wagon, because she knew that, whatever Alyard had said, she was not capable of using the weapon effectively. Then she went with her father to where Alyard and Henry were. Ord had not brought the rifle. They got Henry upright but his body was limp, his head hanging slackly, and together they went stumbling the way they had come. Alyard, now standing, and with his blood-dripping arm, followed them.

At the wagon, Hanni came at once to help with her brother. They lowered him as gently as they could and propped him against one of the big wheels. Sarah, her brown skirts blood-smeared, turned to help Alyard but he made a small gesture indicating that he could manage, and said, 'Give me the Winchester your pa had.' She fetched the rifle.

'There's one in the chamber,' Ord said. Sarah took up the carbine and handed it to her pa. Ord levered it, then propped it against the wheel alongside Henry.

Lilah was underneath the wagon and Hanni told her to stay there. Hanni herself was fetching cloths to try to stanch the flow of blood from Henry. Alyard, observing Henry, thought that whatever she did was not going to make any difference. Stiffly he took the

Sanchez rifle in one hand and, though his vision was not at all good and he was in pain, went several yards away from the wagon and stopped. Slowly then he turned full circle, staring out at the shifting yellow curtain. How long he would be capable of offering any sort of effective defence Alyard had no idea. He thought it might not be long. There followed a period of inactivity from those who had been harassing them. They did not come. Alyard had got down on one knee, the rifle resting across the other. Sarah came. She just reappeared alongside him.

'Henry's real bad. Pa says we got to get him to Doell's Ferry as soon as we can.'

Alyard nodded. But it was a pipe dream. A drawn-out yell caused them to turn in time to see the fearsome Joseph Small Bear, wearing only cavalry pants and with the coloured headband and loose, flying black hair come swinging in towards the wagon, catching Ord flat-footed. As horse and rider went rushing by, Ord staggered against the wagon's side a bloodied line down shoulder and chest where the Indian's knife had striped him. Joseph Small Bear's way. Risking his warrior's skin, drawing blood, vanishing, prolonging the anxiety. He would come again without warning. 'God alone help Ord,' Alyard thought, 'if that bastard takes him alive.' Alyard then thought he saw the shadow of a horseman some fifty feet away and thought about shooting, then didn't do it. He needed a more certain target.

Lilah had come out from under the wagon, looking for her sister. Ord, though in some distress, was again trying to help Hanni with Henry. They were intent upon getting him up on the wagon. Bob Chapin came bursting out of a billow of dust, and from another direction, Joseph Small Bear. Hanni had just got up on the wagon-step when she turned her head to see Chapin sweeping in, leaning down to grab Lilah. The girl screamed, twisting away, and Hanni, jumping down, now had the Schofield. Holding it in both hands she cocked it and fired, the pistol bucking upwards, and Chapin went riding on. Hanni shook her head. Lilah ran to her.

Alyard, one-handed, shot at the crouching Indian but it was the horse that he hit. Joseph Small Bear leaped from it as the animal skidded wildly and went down in boiling dust. With the help of Sarah, Alyard managed to lever the Winchester and waited, but the Indian had gone. Blinking gritty eyes, breathing hard, Alyard watched Ord take the carbine, walk to the thrashing horse that had been the Indian's, and shoot it.

Now Joseph Small Bear was back. No one saw him until he was very nearly atop those at the wagon, and he and Ord Fielder, closing and grappling, went down hard, rolling over and over, wrestling fiercely. Now some of the fury that had been building up in Ord Fielder lent strength to an already strong man. Maybe it came as a shock to Joseph Small Bear but it did not take him long to recover.

Alyard could not do anything about it, not only because he could never have got a clear shot without putting Ord in grave danger, but because his sight was not good and even half kneeling as he was, he was unsteady. Blinking, he watched the grabbing, rolling figures near the wagon. If to begin with there had been a knife in the Indian's hand it was not there now.

Hanni, Lilah with her, had her back pressed against the wagon. Chapin had not come back. Not yet, anyway. Now, somehow, the fighters had come lurching to their feet, and while the Indian was seeking to grab hold of Ord again, the farmer was punching at the other man, and to some effect. It was a mode of fighting that was foreign to Joseph Small Bear and this time, without his knife, he did not have the confidence he had shown in the sandy alley in Bethane, up against an inept cowboy.

The Indian began retreating, Ord

following up, his heavy forearms pumping out. Suddenly Joseph Small Bear turned and ran. He must have been aware that Alyard was across to his right for he veered away. What he did not see was that immediately Ord had gone staggering to the wagon and had grabbed the carbine. Chest heaving, shirt all but torn off, Ord planted his boots firmly and raised the short-barrelled weapon. Joseph Small Bear, on the point of vanishing into the dust, at the bang of the carbine, was thumped forward, his arms splaying, as though he might have been in the act of diving into water. Down he went, tumbling over and over, Ord blundering after him, reloading as he went. The Indian was trying to crawl away but it was mostly in his mind. He was going nowhere. Face taut with fury, Ord shot him again.

They waited but Bob Chapin did not come. Nor did they see Jack Drago. Ord, Hanni and Sarah, who had gone to help, got Henry up on the wagon.

Eventually they did it. Alyard, too, went to the wagon and was helped up and inside it. He wedged himself in, near the back. Ord handed him the carbine, fetched the Winchester and gave him that, too. A few more of the Fielders' possessions were abandoned to the flats.

Presently the wagon moved on, Hanni kneeling at Henry's side. Doell's Ferry had been talked about again. Presumably while Henry was still clinging to life there was still a sliver of hope. Or so they preferred to believe.

Sarah had come, barely able to get by her mother and Henry, and had cleaned and bound up Alyard's arm and side. The dark-clad man's whiskered, hang-moustached face seemed more gaunt than ever.

To Ord he had said, 'But for Henry, I'd have been left to bleach, back there.' Ord in return had stared at him silently. It had sounded as though Alyard might have been taking care to put something on record.

Finally, Ord had asked outright, 'What the hell is it, Tom, 'twixt you an' Henry?'

As the seconds went by it became clear that Alyard would give no answer. The time for that question had passed. Ord did not press it.

When, eventually, they came to the end of Deadman's Flats and with them the last of the driving dust, passing on to undulating, grassy terrain, and were only a few hours away from Doell's Ferry, Hanni made a little sound, then covered Henry's face. She went struggling forward to tell Ord. Hanni wept, then, and Lilah; but not Sarah, who seemed numb and beyond tears. She came easing back, scarcely looking at the covered-over body of Henry, to sit silently with Alyard. He put his good arm around her narrow shoulders and she leaned her weight against him and after a little time, slept.

Sarah awoke only because Ord had brought the wagon to a hurried stop. A rider on a slowly-walking horse was angling in towards them. Some way off they recognized Bob Chapin. Stiffly Alyard climbed down and Sarah handed him the carbine. The rider continued his approach.

Alyard called, 'Hold up, Bob!'

Still Chapin came on. Both of his hands were visible. He was holding only the reins. Thirty feet from the wagon he did stop but it was more the decision of the horse than the rider. Chapin had a lot of blood on him and he was having trouble focusing. Slowly he extended one gloved hand towards them. His mouth opened but for a start no words came. Then, 'Ord . . . Sarah . . . I . . . ' His head rolled sideways and he fell off the horse.

Ord got down and walked across to him. Very soon the farmer straightened and came back and shook his head. Hanni covered her face with her hands. It was she who had fired the Schofield at Bob Chapin and had not truly expected to hit him.

Ord said, 'It was Bob started it.

Mebbe them other fellers kinda took a-holt of it, but he didn't do nothin' to stop 'em. An' then he took part. He coulda kilt us all.' There was still no sign of Jack Drago, nor was there to be. They did not set eyes on him again. Dead, probably, somewhere out on the flats. And Ord said, 'Henry's dead, because o' what Bob done. He was a good man, an' he's dead.'

Alyard was not looking at Ord or at Hanni. There was nothing that he could say to them that would not cause more pain. Henry had gone and he had taken all the demons of his past with him. Plenty of them, no doubt. But none of them worse than those that would have appeared to him in the aftermath of one occurrence. A Union foraging party, ranging the enemy countryside as a regiment paused in its advance, ambushed by local civilians. Shot down and thrown in a ditch. The regiment had found them and buried them but had not immediately moved on.

Four raggy Confederate prisoners had been brought out and had been shot. Angry reprisal. Regrettable. But once the sound of the musketry had died away across the fields, too late for recriminations. Leaving, the firing-party had engaged no other eyes. Names had been remembered though, one of them, Pedderson. A sergeant. A tough man. Just the sort of man to lead the firing party. Under orders. Ours not to reason why. One of several names nonetheless salted away. Some from that party had not survived the war. Then pure chance had brought the name Pedderson to the ears of a once-captain in the Confederate Cavalry, one of whose kinsmen had been among those led out before the drawn-up blue lines.

So Alyard had come looking further and had found Henry, the ex-sergeant, now a man with but one foot. And then, unexpectedly, there had been this farm girl that Alyard's eyes had been drawn back to again and again. Yet, in spite of it, all across Deadman's Flats, Henry had been carrying the death card. Unknowingly? Or, deep down, revealed in his black suspicion of Alyard, had he known all along that his nemesis had come riding, after all that time? Now Alyard would never know.

The false fronts of Doell's Ferry were now cut sharply against the skyline.

'We'll bury Uncle Henry there,' Sarah said.

Alyard looked at her and nodded, covered her hand with one of his. Merely a part of the past now, Henry. The regiment had moved on.

THE END